THE DEMONS THEY FORGED

A GOTHIC GROVE NOVELLA

JA GEORGE

GOTHIC GROVE WORLD

Gothic Grove Series

Gothic Grove
Heavy is the Crown
The Demons They Forged
Ruined Kingdom (coming early 2025)

CONTENT WARNINGS AND TRIGGERS WARNINGS

This is a dark paranormal romance with MF, MMFM and everything in between. Do you expect anything less from Kallen?

If you are at all disturbed or triggered by spice, dark content or the paranormal – do not read. For real, turn back now – this book isn't for you. This book contains adult content and is intended for readers 18+.

Please note the following are all present: anxiety, general love of stabbing, torture, discussion of child SA (off page), human trafficking (off page), SA (off page and not of main characters), revenge, spicy times directly post unaliving people, use of drugs and alcohol, grief, and preganancy loss (not directly mentioned but illuded to).

As I am only human, there is a chance I missed a TW/CW. Please take care of yourself and be mindful of your triggers as you read.

Other warnings include: blood play, biting, impact play, voyeurism, foursome, edging, knotting, and pierced peens. This book is not meant to be a guideline to any sexual activities nor should it be used to reflect healthy relationships.

If you encounter errors in the book OR have other triggers you feel should be added please reach out to the author and not Amazon. Author email: <u>authorjageorge@gmail.com</u>

It is important to note I use some language that is not my first language; I've done my best to make sure I'm using it accurately. Should you notice a mistake, please let me know so I can correct it.

AUTHOR'S NOTE

The timeline of this book spans through book two. You'll notice crossover with events within Heavy is the Crown while reading this novella. Please note you should read Heavy is the Crown prior to this, as it does contain spoilers. Kallen's story is dark; she's morally gray and has no interest in being anything other than that. She'll make choices you may not love, but my hope is you can understand the motivation behind them. This novella also introduces her mate who is president of a motorcycle club. I have done my best to research MCs and gain knowledge of bikes but I'm only human, and I'm in no way an expert. Honestly I wouldn't even say I'm expert-adjacent, but I have done my best.

PRONUNCIATION GUIDE

Kallen Kal-in
Demon *Dee-min*
Dios *D-ohs*
Harrowlena *Hair-oh-len-a*
Astrea *A-stray-a*
Ciaran *Kure-in*
Oisin *Oh-is-sin*
Jackson *Jaxs-son*
Rucker *Ruck-her*
Reaver *Ree-va-her*

Translations
mo chreach bheag My little hellion (Irish)
Deamhan demon (Irish)

PLAYLIST

The Summoning- Sleep Token
American Horror Show- Snow White
Strange Love- Hansley
RIP- Neoni
Your Love Feat. Roniit- One True God
Unholy- Kayla King
Bad Girlfriend- Theory of a Deadman
Cola- Lana Del Rey
What It Cost- Bad Omens
Ava Maria- Tommee Proffitt and Stanaj
I Know Places (Taylors Version)- Taylor Swift
Eat the Acid- Kesha
You can't stop me- Andy Mineo

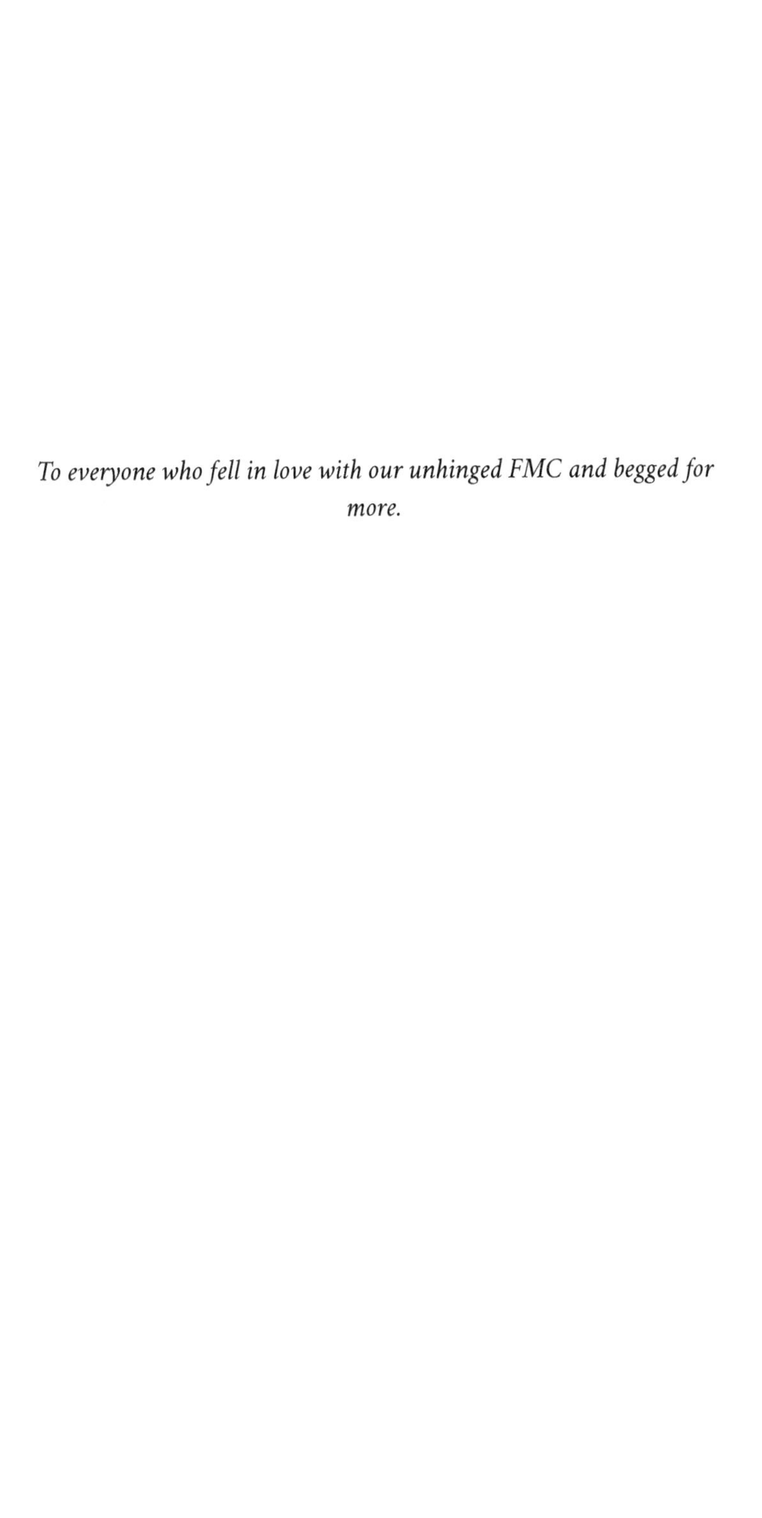

*To everyone who fell in love with our unhinged FMC and begged for
more.*

Formatting by: Mads at Breathless Lit (@breathlesslitpa)
Editing by: Kendra, Spice Me Up Editing
Cover Design By: Sam (damnfinesam.com)

ONE

Kallen

"You seem to be under the impression that I'm not a threat, given I do not have The Harbinger magic," I say as I grip the wolf by the throat. My sharpened nails dig into his skin. I pull him close, his eyes wild as he tries to shift to beast form. "I survived *centuries* without that magic, before and after its creation. You don't think I picked up some other tricks? Other ways to defend myself?" His whole body trembles, panic coursing through his veins. I savor the taste like a fine wine.

The bar around us is silent, everyone poised on a hair trigger. My eyes briefly track the sea of shifters looking at me.

Outside I can hear seagulls and ship horns. The briny smell of water is infiltrating the shit clubhouse I found this pack in. The scent attempts to cover up the smell of vomit and wet dog.

Fucking wolf shifters.

The idea of my mate being stuck in a shifter's body bothers me to no end.

The Feral Riders MC clubhouse is little more than a drug den. The windows are either busted in or covered in thick garbage backs to block out light. The wolves occupying it all look to be addicted to some type of substances, most likely Eufori given the smell.

The wolf in my grip squirms, the scent of urine now infiltrating my nose. I roll my eyes. "Gods, you could have made this so much easier on yourself."

Sweat drips down my temple from holding myself back for so long. I enjoy the carnage. The need to create it, bathe in it, embrace it floods me. The weeks of looking for my mate have forced me to hold back, my skin crawling with the need to feel blood slipping through my fingers. I feel like a junkie looking for a fix.

"Can't shift, can you?" I say to the room. "Fun little piece of magic I found from a witch a few decades ago. She was able to cast far enough to keep people from shifting. It was a lost art really; another magical line that died out because of greed." I look down at the man in front of me who made the mistake of thinking I was just another pair of tits he could take. "The issue with people like you is you are never thinking things through. You don't think of the repercussions, never using the right head - if you know what I mean. I hope that your pack will learn from your mistake." I push my magic into my hand gripping his throat before digging in and ripping his jugular out. Blood begins spraying me like warm summer rain.

Looking at my bloody hand with fascination before licking some of it off, I smile out at the crowd, "Now then… is anyone going to tell me where I can find The Primal Knights?"

Sitting in the shit motel across from the harbor, I wash the blood from my hands, the water turning a rusted color as it goes down the drain. It hadn't taken long for them to tell me where my query was, but I had stopped short of traveling the short distance and instead grabbed a room in this dump. It looks like it hasn't been cleaned in close to a decade, with stains on the carpet that appear suspiciously like blood and mold on the tile in the bathroom. I had no interest in staying overnight here. However, I needed a spot to calm down and to wash the blood off.

Splashing water on my face, I began to scrub, the splatter slowly flaking off my skin until eventually my face is clear. My hair, however, is another story. The blood stands out against the white, but with how dirty the shower is, I refuse to strip down and risk getting some infectious disease. I've spent enough time in disgusting places. Letting out a dramatic sigh, I flip my head over and attempt to wash it out in the sink. Realizing it's a lost cause, I instead bundle it into a messy bun.

Behind me, from the darkness, I feel my Hellbeast prowl into the room. Its luminous eyes rake over me, making sure none of the blood they scent is mine.

"Hello, my little beasty," I say as I throw my arms around his neck. He nuzzles me for a moment before pulling away and sitting back on his hind legs. My earliest memory is of the dark pups materializing in my room. My mother had lost her shit.

Ironically, she called me a Harbinger of death when she saw

me snuggled into the pile of black fur, and in the end, that's what I became.

Demon

Her hair hangs in black strings in front of her face, matted down in parts where the thick locks have collected the gore of her latest kill. She looks more like an animal than a human crouched on the ground. Her blood-crusted fingernails dig into the dirty brick ground. Deep within the coven catacombs, the members of the founding families stand around the magic circle they've caught her in.

"Do you have any remorse for what you've done?" Arthur Mori asks her. "You killed innocent members of the families of the community!"

The laugh that breaks free of her mouth is nothing short of unhinged, the sound bouncing around the dimly lit room like a spectator. She clutches her sides as the laughter keeps bubbling out at the audacity of these people.

"She's clearly gone mad." This comes from a Fairmore witch.

"This is mercy. She should have been put down long ago," says another witch. The woman's head finally snaps up as she looks around the room.

"Madness?" she croaks out, her throat parched from being held for days without water. "Madness was when you chose to murder my mate." The word visibly pains her, as if her chest is cracking in half. The grief is blinding through her dark eyes.

"You have no proof of these allegations, Kallen." Her head jerks towards Arthur; like a broken doll, her movements are off-kilter. Kallen's eyes are wide, as though she knows what led her here. Knows she was lost the moment she did that blood spell.

A howl in the distance startles the witches, "Jumpy, aren't you? Do my pets bother you?" The sound of Hellbeasts in the distance grows louder and more ferocious. As if they've caught a fresh kill, the sounds send a collective chill through the room.

"Enough of this!" someone shouts out. "We know she is guilty, we should kill her!"

Arthur smiles and holds his hand up to silence the murmurs. "We cannot kill her, not with the powers she has gained. However, we will split her soul from the body, power from the soul, and keep her contained within the bodies of one of our own. Dormant and never allowed to hunt us again."

She tilts her head to the side. "You sure that'll hold me, Arty boy?"

His smile is evil, pure evil. Someone like Arthur's only purpose is power for himself; it can't be any shock when he picks his own family to hold her soul. Her eyes cast around the circle until they land on a man in the back, a vampire. A smile creeps over her face, hidden to the room by her hair.

No one pays attention to her as she begins to scratch her finger-nails down her arm, drawing enough blood to imbue with magic. The witches in the room are warded against such magic, but the vampire? No. He has no such protection. She sends her magic out towards him in fine particles that no one can track. And when the magic settles on him, she looks relieved and doesn't fight as they begin to cast the spell.

***

(The Summoning- Sleep Token)

I jolt upward, breathing heavily as I gather my surroundings. Heavy guitar riffs snake their way under the door. People giggle as they run past my closed door before I hear another slam down the hall. The clubhouse walls do little to block out any sounds. After many nights listening to Dios or Rucker fucking someone in the next room, I've grown used to it. I can't seem to sleep without the loud noises now.

There was a time you could only sleep with the sounds of nature.

Grabbing the joint next to my bed, I take a long drag as I

swing my legs off the side and head into the bathroom. It's a desperate attempt to ignore what the dream is attempting to drag up. My chest glistens with sweat in the yellowing bathroom light as I turn the small shower on. Visions of my mate losing her mind continue to play over and over. Nightmares I can handle, they are a companion I've grown used to. But the visions? They are a personal form of torture. It's why I keep a joint next to my bed now, why I'm rarely sober when I fall asleep.

The spot that held my bond, which has sat empty for years, pings with pain and I absently rub at it before shoving my ginger hair back into a bun. At this point the pain is a constant for me, never easing in all the years since our separation.

Her curse was to be locked away; mine was to come back over and over without her.

I'm not sure which is worse.

Grabbing my leather cut off the back of my chair, I swing it over my body as I exit into the dark hallway. The Primal Knights MC clubhouse holds most of the brothers in the club along with a few extra prospects. We have our bar and kitchen that is normally stocked full in the front with rooms lining the back hallway. It had been passed down to me by my father, the old president, after he died.

No, after he was murdered.

Rage and grief intertwine as the thought moves through me; my father being killed is in a long line of wrongs that need to be righted someday. Despite our tense relationship at the end, the loss is still a deep wound I can't seem to let go of.

Before the thoughts can overtake me I see our prospect walking back with one of the club whores. "Yo. Where is Dios?" I ask, taking another hit of the joint in my hand. The scent of marijuana blooms into the hallway, overpowering the smell of booze for a moment. The girl kisses his neck and starts to palm his cock in front of me, her eyes locked directly on my own.

My dick stays soft; I have no interest in hooking up with these two.

"The Sea Dog," he groans.

Shaking my head, I tell him thanks as I head to my bike. He's a good kid and one I hope to patch in fully soon, but he's also impulsive. His wolf is untamed and the closer he gets to his heat the harder he looks for a mate.

"Lainey was looking for you," he shouts after me. "I sent her towards the bar."

Biting back the groan, I tip my head in thanks. Lainey was a mistake. She started as a way to ease the loneliness with a bonus being that she is the daughter of a local gang. A gang that could give us the numbers when we went against the Feral Riders. Or if the Dragons ever came looking for retribution.

Lainey wants power; she may be a puppet for her father but deep down she wants her own slice of this city. She thinks becoming my old lady is the way to achieve that. Little does she know she'll never hold that title. So long as I live, I'll hold the silent vigil for the loss of my mate all those lifetimes ago.

My boots crunch on the gravel parking lot, the sounds of laughter dimming as my ride comes into view. The sleek black piece of machinery seems to gobble up the light around it, pulling a smile from me. Slinging my leg over it, I switch the key on, allowing the engine to rumble to life.

This.

This right here is one of the only times that I feel free. The visions and nightmares can't catch me when I ride – it's just me and my wolf.

The Sea Dog flashes its neon lights in the dimly lit sky of Gothic Grove as my bike rumbles to a stop. I can see the bikes of my vice president and sergeant at arms already parked along with half a dozen other pack members. The smell of garbage and seawater invades my nostrils as I step off my escape. Gothic Grove has always been a dank city, even before Alexi took over, but now it's even worse. It cannot govern itself, regardless of what its citizens may say. And thus far, no one has been strong enough to take the lead. Just groups scrambling for dominance.

Lainey's father has continued to try, but they cannot get a foothold to stand on. Some believe Drago would step in but so far he's made no move to expand his empire outside his club and Eufori business. Alexi's son has also been seemingly quiet since the prison was destroyed, having disappeared after Samhain. The vampires are running amok through the city, the witches have all but vanished, and the shifters are in a constant battle. The entire city is on the edge of a blade ready to tip over.

Shoving open the door to the tavern, I'm greeted with laughter and loud music. The air is filled with smoke and even from here, I can see the group is fucking wasted. I see Dios, my sergeant at arms, face down in some pussy, the girl's head thrown back in pleasure. His own hand is gripping his thick cock as he pumps it up and down. Dios enjoys exhibitionism and voyeurism, really everything and isn't shy about it. He's opened my eyes to a whole new world, and part of me wishes Kallen was here to see it all. To do it all with me.

Letting the door shut behind me, I take a deep breath. The air has a tingle of electricity in it, a scratching in the back of my mind as a familiar scent floats under it all. My brain attempts to place the scent, to pull it deeper and identify it as my eyes shift around the rest of the establishment, trying to pinpoint where it's coming from. Frowning, I see a woman perched at the bar. Her back is to me but her white hair stands out brightly among the masses. Something about her is pulling me in that direction, a deep need to turn her around and see her eyes. She's calling to me, this stranger. My wolf growls low, wanting to scent her.

Just as I go to take a step forward, Lainey's voice drags my attention away, her voice like nails on a chalkboard. "I missed you," she purrs, looping her arms around my neck and pulling me in for a kiss. Her lips land on my cheek. I don't miss the way her eyes narrow into annoyed slits at my ability to dodge her.

"Sorry baby. I'm here now, though." I lean down to her and graze my lips across her forehead. I can only toe the line for so long with her before she'll go to her father. And the last thing I need is Cornelius to get pissed at us.

She lights up with a smile and tucks her thin form against mine. "It's okay. You're forgiven," she giggles, pushing her hands into the back pockets of my jeans. I allow my eyes to draw back to the bar, feeling a sense of loss when I see the white-haired girl is gone.

Untamed and unchecked frustration pulses through me; an irrational anger that I missed the girl grating me. When Lainey paws at me, my wolf wants to rip free from my skin. The feeling of her touching me makes my skin feel tight and uncomfortable. Gripping her hair roughly and pulling it back, I shove her to the floor, ignoring her outraged cry.

"What the fuck, Demon!" she growls, looking up at me from her knees.

I unzip my pants, allowing my cock to spill out. I grip it hard, stroking it up and down, coaxing it to hardness with no regard to anyone else around. "Suck it," I growl before shoving past her lips.

I can't help but picture the white-haired girl at my feet instead of Lainey. I image how her mouth would feel, how I would fuck her hard until she was gagging and crying. I can imagine how turned on she would be, her cunt dripping from the act of sucking me off. The scent of her would drive everyone wild, dying to touch what's *mine*.

With no warning my balls draw up and I rip my dick from her mouth, cum spraying her in the face. A low growl pulls from my chest as my eyes close so I can continue picturing that white-haired goddess.

"Are you kidding me right now!?" she screeches, ripping me from my daydream. "Do you know how long this is going to take to get out of my hair?!"

I don't offer an apology as I tuck my spent dick back into my pants. Her nostrils flare at my silence as she pushes herself back to her feet.

"Are you going to take care of me?" she asks, projecting her voice across the bar. The desperate attempt to save face disgusts me.

"No," I reply and push past her roughly.

"I'm telling my father about this!"

I let out a chuckle as I grab the whiskey bottle from behind the bar, taking a long swig of it. "You're going to tell your father how you let me fuck your face in the middle of the bar like a whore? Or are you going to tell him about all the other guys you let fuck that pussy of yours?" She pales at the last statement. "Yeah, I know you've been fucking around. So don't try to threaten me, because you'll fucking lose."

No one says anything at the display, the bar quickly resuming its normal boisterous evening. But I don't miss the hard glare Rucker cuts me or the concerned look on Dios's face.

"Yeah because you won't touch me!" she screeches. "My heat is coming and you won't help me, I'm in need, Demon." Her voice hits a fever pitch and I have to close my eyes against the sound. "You aren't worthy of the title of alpha or president!"

The statement snaps me, my wolf surging forward and a loud growl ripping from me. Lainey goes wide-eyed, stepping backwards from me. The bar goes silent, the wolves around us responding to their alpha. "You will never fucking be my old lady, Lainey, get that in your head. I have no interest in knocking you up either. So find someone else to spend your heat with." I step closer again, towering over her. "And speak to me like that again, you'll be going back to your father in pieces."

Her eyes well but I don't miss the way her lips start to pull into a sneer. "You don't have the numbers, I'm going to tell him about this and you'll change your tune." She backs away slowly before scurrying out of the bar.

"Demon. . ." Rucker slowly approaches. I cut him a glare.

"Don't." I sound more wolf than human. I'm on edge, my temper exploding quicker than usual. Something has set me off, and it wasn't Lainey.

I turn around and lean against the bar, pulling more of the whiskey from the bottle. "You normally don't lose it with Lainey's bullshit." Dios's sultry, dark voice comes from the left. The only one brave enough to approach me.

"I'm in a bad mood," I say. "Just drop it."

He doesn't argue, just shrugs, before leaning over and grabbing a beer from the well. It's one of the best parts of Dios; he can read the room and doesn't push.

TWO

The vampire I used the blood magic on is less
helpful than I had hoped.
He holds no power.
But he will.
I will make sure that he is my tool to help
destroy the covens.
-Personal Journal of Kallen

Kallen

It took everything in me to not kill the bitch hanging on my mate. I'm downright proud of myself for walking straight out of the bar. Wiping my knife off on my pants, I put it back in my boot. The witch at my feet had sung so lovely as I tortured the information needed from him. Did he need to be tortured? Probably not. But I deserved a reward for not painting the bar red with that little slut's blood.

Lainey Fentraway. The girl who is currently as close to engaged as you can get, without actually being engaged, to my mate. Cornelius Fentraway had agreed to provide manpower to the Primal Knights should they ever need it, but only after his daughter Lainey had taken a liking to the alpha of the pack and president of the club. *My* mate. The up-and-coming wannabe gang leader saw an opportunity and took it. Having the Knights in his pocket would be extremely helpful in the future.

Rumor around the city is that the Primal Knights had sided with Alexi at some point, the vampire using them for a more covert way of killing. Particularly after his dragon was taken from him. But after Demon's father was killed by the Feral Riders, Demon left the vampires and tried to turn the club around. Enter Lainey.

From the sound of it, Lainey was using her status with her father to manipulate Demon into wife-ing her up.

"Which simply will not do," I mutter, stepping over the dead witch.

The thick fog in the city streets lays over the asphalt like a weighted blanket as my black combat boots carry me out of the alleyway onto the sidewalk. The main drive of the city is seemingly quiet, and I tuck my white hair deep into the large hood of my sweatshirt. Visibility may be shit, but my snow-white hair isn't exactly inconspicuous. While I enjoy being notorious, anonymity is key when one wants to murder the head of a gang.

Noise from my movements is muffled as I meander through the sparsely crowded streets. This time of day is an odd transition for most; the hours when it's too late for socially acceptable activities but too early for nefarious deeds where one would prefer to be cloaked by darkness. Give it another hour and people will be lined up down the block for club access, dealers will be out on the streets, and the distant rumble of street racing will vibrate through the tall skyscrapers.

A few blocks from my destination I weave a glamor over my body, a mousy brown-haired youth with sad eyes. Another piece of information I gathered is that Fentraway Sr. seems to like his girls young and his boys even younger. It seems that young individuals are often sent to his penthouse but are never seen again. It hits on an old wound, one from my previous life that has never quite healed.

Adjusting my hair, I step back into the street and quickly stride up to the lobby of his penthouse. I breathe deeply, channeling the girl from so long ago that my mate found on the side of the road, as I step into the lobby.

"Excuse me," I whisper to the doorman. "I'm here for Mr. Fentraway." The bean pole of an old man narrows his eyes at me.

"Who sent you?" he asks.

Biting my lip, I toy with the hem of my skirt, "Lainey sent me. She said he would take care of me."

The lust in the doorman's eyes is undeniable. I watch as he moves back behind the desk and presses a button, a loud buzz echoing in the lobby before I hear the locks disengage from the large glass doors that separate me from the elevators.

"Come on honey," the guard says sweetly, directing me to walk in front of him towards the elevators. "He's up in the penthouse." I nod, sniffling to add to the innocent, nonthreatening look I'm going for.

As I scoot past, the guard ghosts a hand down the small of my back, breathing deeply as he does so.

Fucking pig is scenting me.

My hand twitches, magic burning through me as images of his death intrude into my mind.

He is going to die a painful death.

Pressing the button to the elevator, his eyes trail over me.

The smile on his face feels oily. When the door opens I move in quickly, throwing magic behind me to keep him in place. His body sways a bit at the force before he meanders off, confusion playing over his old face. I let the mask slip for just a moment, rage burning behind my eyes. His mouth opens as if to shout, but it's cut off by my Hellbeast closing its jaws around his neck and biting down.

The doors close to the satisfying sound of his bones snapping.

The ride goes quickly, the doors opening into a large open-concept room. The white marble floors are pristine. A small smile creeps over my face — white marble like this shows blood so well..

"Oh my, you are a beauty." The deep voice comes from my left. Turning towards it, Cornelius ambles out of the shadows. His shaggy dark hair is slicked back from his face exposing his dark eyes. His face is clean-shaven and oddly youthful. The body hidden beneath his dark suit looks sturdy and muscular; he's the exact opposite of what one would imagine a man like him would look like.

Though I've learned, the most dangerous monsters come in the prettiest packages.

"Come in, dear." He gestures to me, beckoning me forward.

Stepping closer I keep my eyes locked on the ground, fully committed to my roll until I know we are alone. The twins are searching the rooms; Lark and Cora are the two of my beasts that do the best stealth work.

Stopping directly in front of his shiny black shoes, I allow him to tip my gaze up to him. "Take off your coat and get comfortable, lovely. Daddy will take care of you." I hold back vomiting on him and slip off the thin jacket, exposing the tight tank top I chose under it. He clearly adjusts the bulge in his pants.

Don't roll your eyes, don't roll your eyes.

Breathing through my nose, I bite my lip and offer a shy smile. "Thank you, sir. I was so scared of those wolves but Lainey promised me I would be safe here."

The mention of his daughter's name does little to quell his arousal; if anything, he has an even bigger smile spread across his face. "My Lainey is a smart girl, always sending me those who need to be taken care of." Dropping his hand from my chin, he guides me over to the long black couch that seems to overlook the open windows. On a clear day, I'm sure he has a spectacular view.

Such a pity I'll need to burn this place, it could have been a lovely abode.

Sitting down, he pulls me onto his lap, his erection digging into me. His fingers delicately stroke my bare thigh, each pass pushing him closer to the edge of my skirt and beyond. "Now, did Lainey tell you what you would need to do to stay here?"

"I…" My eyes dart around the room in an unsure moment, allowing the man to think I'm afraid. He tutts and presses his nose to my neck.

"Shhh it's okay, no need to be frightened." Just as his hand breaches the edge of my skirt I feel the ripple of darkness from the twins returning. It's the confirmation I need that we are all clear.

"Thank fuck," I growl as I push to stand, allowing the glamor to drop.

His face goes from confusion to outrage rapidly. He moves to stand, reaching for his gun. Swiftly I push him back down and straddle him. "Nope. You aren't going anywhere, silly goose." I note his arousal is long gone. "What? Because I'm not a kid you aren't hot for me? I'm offended."

"Who are you?" he growls as he struggles against me, my magic adding an extra layer of hold.

"Hmm…I suppose you would know me as the former Harbinger. Now, you can call me Kallen."

Cornelius goes pale, his skin taking on a deathly white hue as he sees the Hellbeasts emerge from the darkness, Laoch leading the pack of three. "I'm sure we can come to some sort of arrangement, whatever it is you think I did. I can pay you!"

I roll my eyes at the predictability. "Sadly, my disgusting friend, your daughter touched what was mine."

"Lainey?" His eyes draw down in confusion.

I lean close to him, my mouth right next to his ear. "She touched my mate. Demon."

He struggles, pulling away from me. "You can have him! Kill her if she's touched him, I wasn't the one who did it!"

Leaning back, I shake my head in disappointment, "How fucking predictable. Throwing your daughter under the bus. Don't worry, I'll make sure both of you pay."

"HELP!" Cornelius screams, thrashing against me. "SOMEONE HELP!"

A soft chuckle pushes from me. "My friends made sure no one would bug us. Now. . . let's have some fun."

It takes far less time than I had planned to slaughter the worthless man in front of me, his blood now a splattered mess across my face and body. He had screamed until his voice gave out as I finally ripped his cock free of his body. Sadly he died right after, the pool of blood at my feet spreading out rapidly as his body lays at an awkward angle.

"He deserved a much longer torture," I pout. Stepping over the ripped-off cock, I walk into the massive kitchen glancing around before spotting the liquor cabinet. Pulling free some whiskey I pop the bottle open, drinking a shot as I meander through the giant penthouse, the bottle hanging loosely at my side. The air is quiet save for my footsteps; not even the city noise breaches the windows.

"Fucker probably has it soundproofed."

Peeking into each room, I catalog every ounce of shit the man has. When I arrive at the last room I glance in, bile rising to my throat. It's decorated in pale blues and very clearly decorated with the intent of having a younger guest stay. I step in, grinding my teeth together, furious that he is dead and I can't drag out his torture for even longer.

This could have been me. I suppress a shudder at the thought, locking the memories away.

I sit down on the bed, my hands touching the scratchy sheets.

Warm.

The sheets are warm.

My head snaps up as I realize I'm not alone. He had someone else here. Glancing towards the empty hallway I watch as Lark and Cora materialize, Cora tilting her head towards a closet. I had told my beasts to find out if there were threats in the apartment. Whoever was in the closet wasn't a threat in their eyes.

"Next time tell me someone is here," I whisper harshly at the two. Lark rolls her eyes at me as Cora snaps playfully. I shake my head at the two.

Pushing up to my feet, I casually walk towards the closed door, stopping just outside of it. A soft whimper sneaks out from under it. I open the door slowly; while they may not be a threat, that doesn't mean they won't try to do something stupid. Cornered animals lash out even if they are normally the tamest of creatures.

The light of the room blankets the dark space, illuminating a closet with a pile of clothes on the floor. It isn't until my eyes scan up that I see the small shifter pressed against the back wall, his big eyes peering up over his arms wrapped around his knees. His mop of curly blond hair lays in an unruly mess. Another whimper escapes him as he presses further back, as if he hopes the wall will swallow him up. I cock my head to the side as I analyze him, the two of us in an awkward standoff of who will talk first.

"Hi," I say finally. I lower myself down to the ground slowly, kneeling in front of him but allowing enough space so he could push past me if needed. He blinks again rapidly. "My name is Kallen." I think about offering a reassuring smile, but nothing about my smile has ever been reassuring.

The tiny shifter looks past me a bit, as if waiting for someone else to show up. "Are you…" he starts. "Did he send you here?"

Looking down at my nails, I start to rub the blood clean off my fingers. "If you're talking about the twat who is currently in pieces in the living room, he won't be sending anyone in here again." I glance up, the boy's eyes impossibly wide now. "What's your name, little creature?"

"Ari," he says hesitantly.

Pushing up to my feet, I reach my hand out. "Well Ari, you're free to go. The creep out there won't be able to bother you anymore." He looks at my hand but doesn't reach up to take it. "Look, kid, I've got shit to do. At some point someone is going to notice their boss is dead, and I don't really have time to deal with all that bullshit."

He doesn't move, still frozen to the wall. Part of me recognizes I should have patience with him but my skin itches to get back to my mate after waiting for so long. "Whatever, stay here if you want." I mutter, turning to leave. Slowly meandering back out of the disgusting room, I hear the unmistakable scuff of feet once I hit the threshold of the bedroom.

"I have nowhere." His soft voice is barely audible.

Glancing over my shoulder I take in his disheveled appearance. He's severely underweight and doesn't look as if he's showered for a while. The clothing he has on is clearly meant to make him appear younger. "How old are you?"

"21," he replies, still quiet.

Turning to face him, I cross my arms over my chest. "Alright, Ari, come on. You can stick with me; I have some friends who can help." Lark and Cora bleed back into the room from the shadows, the boy freezing up as he eyes the massive beasts. "This is Lark, the other is Cora. They are mine. No one will touch you or hurt you with them around. They also will not hurt you. You are safe with them, and me. Do you understand?"

A quick nod is all I get before I gesture for him to follow. When we walk through the living room, his gasp brings a smile to my face as he takes in the carnage of Cornelius, his body in pieces across the apartment. Turning, I offer him a wicked smile. "This is what happens to people who touch things that are mine. And Ari, you are currently under my protection. So this is what will happen to anyone who touches you or so much as looks at you wrong. Got it?"

The low growl of both my Hellbeasts pull me from the boy, their hackles raising as they push forward to place themselves between us and whatever has set them off. From the kitchen walks out a man, his dark black hair pulled up in a bun and glowing eyes peering out through the darkness. Shoving the small boy behind me, I narrow my eyes at the newcomer still obscured by the shadows.

"Imagine my shock when I came here and someone had already taken care of my problem." His voice is rough, hoarse almost, like he's been yelling for decades.

"I saved you time," I respond, edging Ari back further as the two beasts now press their bodies against either side of us. "We were just leaving."

He doesn't step from the shadows, but when he takes a drag of a cigarette, the cherry lights up his hand enough to see tattoos decorating it. "Who's your friend?" he asks.

"None of your business," I answer rapidly, pulling a

whimper from behind me. "Unless you want to end up like this asshole I suggest you let us leave."

The man steps forward, his body illuminated fully now. His dark suit is pristine, but does nothing to cover up his massive body size. Ari peeks out from behind me, and the man's nostrils flare, his eyes widening a bit. I elbow the boy back behind me, Lark pressing into him tightly.

"You need help, little one?" he asks in that same raspy voice.

I cross my arms over my chest. "I'm taking him somewhere safe. Back the fuck off."

He cuts me with a hard glare before peaking back at Ari. "You need help, you get yourself to Club Eufori. Ask for Kai. Got it?"

My eyes widened a fraction. "You work for Drago?" The man, Kai, snaps his eyes to mine. "Tell him Kallen says hi."

It's my parting words as I open a portal and shove all of us through, flipping my middle finger up at Kai as it closes.

———

Demon

"They say she is an *angel vengadora*. An *avenging* angel," I hear Dios say. Dios fears nothing; he earned the name *El dador de la Muerte* through anointing himself in the blood of our enemies. Some whisper he is a death god, set upon this city as a curse. And yet he crosses himself now as he speaks of her.

"Gothic Grove is nothing but witches and bloodsuckers. It's probably some spurned lover." Rucker, my vice president, says as he picks his nails with his butterfly knife. "You know how pussy gets when it's tossed aside." I frown at his callous tone. He's got his blonde hair completely shaved off and slams the shot of vodka back before grabbing the cool beer in front of him. He's never been the same since Dahlia disappeared.

But Dios continues, undeterred. "I know what you're thinking, but this one is different. They are saying her beauty lures you in and just when you think she is going to have you — BAM. She has some type of magic that no one can go against." He slams a shot back, his one blue eye and one green eye tracking around the bar.

Silence isn't something The Sea Dog Tavern knows. But it's as close to silent as it can be as everyone listens to Dios.

"So what? Why do we care?" Rucker asks before he pounds another shot back.

"She's asking about us," he says. I grab my beer off the bar, the condensation slowly slipping down the side of the glass before I focus my attention on them fully.

"Who did you hear this from?" I ask.

Dios looks over at me before pulling a cigarette out, the flicker of flames giving him a sinister look. "Luke's boys, the ones that survived anyway. Johnny ran into Carla over on 5th Street. He said they got lucky that a good part of the club was on a ride, or everyone may have died."

Rucking throws his shot glass to the ground at the name of the man who took Dahlia, who started us down a path that ended in bloodshed.

"She'd be dead if she walked into that bar. So, not our issue anymore," I say in an attempt to control the rage. "Johnny probably wanted to see if we'd fall for it and show up on their turf." While Johnny is the VP and biggest instigator of all our issues, it's Luke whose blood my wolf wants to dine on. The president of Feral Riders. And the one who killed my father.

And Dahlia got lost in the crossfire of it all.

Of all my regrets, allowing Johnny to get his paws on her is one of my biggest. Her cold eyes looking back at me as Johnny dragged her onto his bike will haunt me until the end of my very long life. The innocent, playful girl gone and replaced by who Johnny molded her into.

My sergeant-at-arms shakes his shaved, tattooed head. "*Es*

lo que pensaba. That's what I thought," he says, his voice pulling me back from the lake of guilt I want to drown in. "They are saying she is, or was, *La Heraldo.* The Harbinger. She controlled their shift and kept them human. And at her beck and call were Hellbeasts."

I let out a loud barking laughing, pushing through the tightness in my chest at the name. Dios raises an eyebrow at me. Of everyone in the club, he is the only one who knows my full story. I have no interest in people finding out who I was to the Harbinger.

Rucker frowns and rolls his eyes. "The Hellbeasts were attached to Alexi's whore, weren't they?" he asks, sloppily pouring another shot. The clear liquid runs over onto the old wooden bar top. His voice slurs slightly, the vodka clearly catching up to him.

"From what I heard, yes. Alexi died in the prison raid," I say. Movement at the door has me glance that way, a group of younger wolves spilling in all laughing. "If he had survived, there is no way she would have."

The packs had heard about a witch taking the whole operation down. Now the prison lay in ruins; a cursed place we all steer very clear of. Even if that large aviary lay empty and smoldering, none of us want to bring that curse down upon our heads if *it* had survived. We all still remember what the harbor looked like after it was unleashed on us and the witches who lived there.

That's his anger without knowing what we did, what we were forced to do.

I swallow down more beer, the last bit now warm. It sits heavy in my stomach, like it's trying to drag me to the ocean floor. Too many memories of the past assault me, forcing me to look in the mirror that shows all the mistakes I've made. Mistakes that haunt me down every hallway I walk.

Frowning, I signal for another beer, the old bartender

nodding as he hands a fresh glass to one of the serving girls. "Hellbeasts are fickle," I say. "They wouldn't transfer to someone else."

They only answered to her, and tolerated me. Images of their dark bodies flash over my mind, attempting to draw me backwards in time. I grind my nails into the palm of my hand, refusing to get pulled backward.

A sickeningly fake female voice penetrates the dim noise of the bar, pulling my attention from Dios, "Demon, honey, we are going to be late for my father's." The fake seduction in the voice has my eye twitching. She bounced back well from our argument; in fact, one would think it never even happened.

Dios rolls his eyes before shooting a disgusted look at her. Lainey moves next to me, her nails scraping down my arm before I can pull away. Her scent clings to my nose, souring the beer in my stomach. "Daddy wanted to see us before my heat starts."

Her shrewd muddy eyes pin me as her rosy lips pull into a pout. The threat is clear. She's expecting to spend her heat with me balls deep in her and knocking her up. The thought makes me want to vomit. This is her retaliation for my outburst.

Out of the corner of my eye, white flashes as more wolves pour into the bar and something pulls in my chest. Turning towards the front door I see a curvy, white-haired woman spill into the bar. Barely catching herself from falling to the ground, she glares at the wolves that shoved her in, the look both chilling and strangely arousing. Her eyes track around and when they meet mine, the world slams to a stop. My chest feels like it's aflame, bursting into life for what feels like the first time. The feeling almost causes me to double over.

The bar falls silent around us, a knowing tension in the air. A predator is here As the girl rights herself two massive black Hellbeasts step up alongside her, their heads towering over her frame. Their form would dwarf all but myself and Dios should we shift. Coarse black fur covers their wolf-like body, teeth bared and leaking deep green poison as they look around with glowing yellow eyes.

Dios utters out a prayer even as he steps up next to me. One of the beasts lets out a guttural growl, the sound vibrating the bar. It moves to position itself in front of the girl, as though she is the most valuable thing in the world to it. My wolf pushes outward; he simmers beneath the surface, stuck behind a cage of magic not of my making. He thrashes against the strange magic.

(American Horror Show- Snow Wife)

"Yeah, sorry. Until I know y'all won't try anything, I'm not letting you shift," she says, glancing down at her nails in a bored move. "It's poor form to kill my *mate's* pack. Or I'm pretty sure it is." She lets out a long sigh before crossing her arms over her ample chest. She cocks her head at Dios. "You smell like Hell magic." He remains silent. She narrows her eyes before a small smirk plays over her lips. "I met a witch recently that smelled like you. She was fun."

My mind is reeling, trying to catch up, when it snags on the word *mate*. Every part of me refuses to allow the ember of hope in my chest to fully catch flame. I let my gaze trace over her body until they meet luminous green orbs that seem to shine. She softens for a moment, almost taking a step towards me, until her eyes zero in on Lainey who is still clutching onto my arm.

"Remove your hands from him." The calm voice sends shivers through me, those green eyes flaming with the promise of death if she doesn't comply.

The dumb bitch on me scoffs, moving in closer to me. "I don't have to do shit, who do you think you are?"

With unnatural speed the white-haired girl is in front of us, pulling Lainey away by her greasy hair. "I'm his fucking *mate*, who do you think you are bitch?"

Lainey dares to laugh, though it sounds unsure and nervous. "I'm his fiancée, he doesn't have a mate. Tell her, Demon!" she demands.

"Kallen?" My voice comes out as a hushed whisper.

"*Deahman.*" The breathy prayer hits me square in the chest. My arm reaches for her without thought, the siren luring me in.

Lainey's annoying voice breaks the spell. "What the fuck, Demon, tell this bitch to let me go!"

Kallen sneers at her, tightening her grip on the dirty hair.

"My daddy will fuck your life up if you don't let me go," Lainey whines, tears springing into her eyes from the pressure no doubt.

Kallen lets out a low chuckle, the sound haunting. "I don't think daddy will be doing anything to me."

Lainey's comment is a reminder that we can't afford to have a war with her father. "Let her go, Kallen." The command ripples out of me and causes her green eyes to flare wide with annoyance before morphing to understanding as she lets go of Lainey.

Lainey smirks. "Yes, *Kallen.* Run along so I can fuck my future husband. We've got to practice for my upcoming heat." She curls back into my chest, my skin crawling in every spot this girl touches.

Kallen's eyes zero in on the hands that are touching my chest before locking eyes with me again. She tilts her head, a predator assessing its prey. Her nostrils flare as she lets out a huff of annoyance and shakes her head. "If you can get him hard, let me know, because all I can smell on him is disgust for you." Lainey goes to surge forward but I pull back on her wrist, keeping her in place.

It's at that point I notice the dried blood staining the white tucked into the messy bun atop Kallen's head and the spots across her neck. My eyes track over the rest of her, cataloging each fleck.

"Are you hurt?"

She smiles wildly. "Nope." She draws out the word, the 'p' popping. "But I can't say the same for Cornelius." She holds my gaze a little longer. "I need a drink; that was one sick fuck." She saunters over to the bar through the sea of shifters she is still holding hostage with her magic. Leaning over the old wooden top, she pushes her ass out as she grabs a fifth from the other side and a shot glass.

"What do you mean?" Lainey shrieks. "Demon, ask her what she means!"

But I can't pull my eyes away from the backside of Kallen. My mouth waters at her round ass. It's aching to have my teeth marks in it. My cock gets hard just thinking about it.

"Oh baby, you're already picturing fucking me aren't you?" Lainey says as she reaches down and cups my cock through my jeans. It's a reckless and desperate move to stake her claim.

In a flash, my mate is in front of us pulling her back. "Tsk, tsk, Lainey. Your father learned the hard way what touching without permission earns. Guess you will too." With a gleeful smile painted on her lips, I watch Kallen shove her other hand through the girl's chest, ripping her heart out. The bloody appendage drops from her hand at the same moment Lainey's body falls to the dirty wood floor with a soft thud.

She wipes the blood on her dark pants, a look of satisfaction playing across her face before looking back up. "Anyone else want to touch what's mine?" I hear Dios utter a curse as he takes in the very dead Lainey at our feet.

The show of savage dominance has my dick hardening in my pants to a painful level. My eyes rake over her thick body. She's wearing tight leather pants that hug her thick thighs and show off her round ass. The black tank top leaves little to the imagination. Her skin is milky white and free of marks or tattoos. Her nails are filed into sharp points and painted black, at least from what I can tell under the blood still coating her.

She isn't anything like my Kallen.

But my Kallen wouldn't fit this life.

I take a small step forward towards her, ignoring the body I step over, "*Mo chreach bheag,* how?"

She scratches the black fur of the beast to her left, its head coming slightly above her own. Its presence only further confirms this is my Kallen. "You didn't think I would let them get away with it, did you?" Her voice shakes with anger. A whirlwind of emotions flash over those strangely luminous emerald eyes before it disappears again. "I've spent a very long time working on our revenge. Lifetimes of hunting those down who hurt us. When I found out you were alive, I came for you instead."

"That's a long time to be hunting people down," I say carefully, my mind doing the mental math of just how long it's been. Just how many lives she's lived.

"Yes, it was. Imagine my shock when I heard you were alive." Anger laces her voice, pent of frustration over what was taken from us. "And imagine how it felt to know you were fucking this piece of trash." She kicks Lainey's heart across the floor. "Not that I'm sex-shaming, but her? Really?"

"A necessary evil," I reply, taking a small, hesitant step towards her.

She simply raises an eyebrow at me, the Hellbeast near us letting out another growl. Its lips pull back and away from its gleaming teeth. I don't back down; at one time these creatures and I held a truce, and I sent a small prayer up to the gods that they still remember that.

"You look different. . ." I hesitate, not wanting her to think I don't enjoy this body. Because fuck, do I enjoy it. I can already picture grabbing handfuls of those soft breasts and how my cock would look slipping into her as I spread those thick thighs.

She shrugs. "The covens tried to trap me, my soul locked away in various witches. This body was donated by Reem Mori." She gestures down.

"Donated?" Rucker asks from behind. The tone isn't missed.

She narrows her eyes at him before focusing back on me. "Some whom I possessed had no awareness when I took over. Their souls blissfully floating away. Others, like Reem, knew. Though no one was as helpful as she was." A deep sadness pulses through her, the green in her eyes turning watery.

I take another step forward, and another, before I've eaten up the small amount of space between us and I'm standing directly in front of her, the scent of blood and sweat invading my nostrils. She smells like death. Without thinking I grab her face, pulling those full lips into mine for a ravaging kiss.

THREE

The bodies of these witches cannot hold me long. Their souls are too fragile to survive. This witch offers up conjuring to reside alongside the realm walking I've brought from the last one. What a lovely surprise that I can collect these powers and carry them forward.
-Personal Journal of Kallen

Kallen (Strange Love-Halsey)

Home. The taste floods my mouth and my chest pulses; that space that sat empty for so long suddenly feels more whole than it has in decades. I dig my hands into his thick hair, keeping his lips pressed against me. Trails of ignited flames move up and down my body until they settle directly in my core. The world begins and ends in this single kiss.

Hungry. I'm fucking hungry for him.

My hands travel his body, taking in the thick panes of muscle hidden under his clothing until they meet the bulge in his jeans.

He pulls back from my mouth, nipping my bottom lip as he rests his forehead against mine. "Oh love, as much as I'd love to continue this, do you think you could release my pack?" he asks as he continues to give me light kisses across my mouth.

I let out a dramatic sigh and drop the magic. I can *feel* the anger vibrating through the room aimed at me. Every wolf is ready to take me apart. I can't blame them, but I've never been one to cower.

Stepping out of his embrace, I smirk at the room around me, "This is my only warning. Fuck around and find out, or leave me be." As if to support my claim, my Hellbeast drops its large head onto my shoulder as its yellow eyes assess the room. Most of the wolves have the decency to look nervous and back away.

They are going to shit when they find out I have a whole pack. I can't help but let a smirk play across my lips.

"You're going to let this bitch come in here and make demands, Demon?! She just started a fucking war!" My gaze zeros in on the younger wolf shifter, my lip curling in disgust as I take in his "fuck boi" energy. This is the type of asshole to drug someone's drink. My magic shoots out in a red arc, pulling his body to me by his neck.

He drops to my feet unceremoniously. Bending down in his face, I offer up an unhinged smile. "Make the mistake of assuming I take orders from anyone, Demon included, and I'll fucking gut you." I grip his face in my hand, squeezing so hard the tips of my nails puncturing his baby smooth skin. "Or maybe *do* make the mistake. Blood turns me on." I lick up the side of his face. Outside, the howls of my beasts echo into the night, and the two here with me answer their call. The chilling melody pulls anyone questioning me into line.

Standing to my full height, I seek out Demon's warmth again and drag his mouth to mine. My tongue slips in to savor his taste before I pull back once more. "And for your information, Cornelius is long dead, along with any men who didn't fall in line."

Demon's hand circles my throat, his eyes devouring me. "No one touches her. And no one fucking disturbs us for the rest of the night. CLEAR OUT!" The command vibrates through the bar, an alpha command. No one argues.

"Pres…" the angry blond one starts to say.

"Unless you want to watch me fuck her right here, you will both get out," Demon growls deeply. "That includes you, Dios. I'm not sharing right now."

My pussy immediately soaks my leggings at the thought of being taken by Demon and Dios.

Fuck I need to make that happen.

"I don't remember you being so kinky. I think I like this version," I moan out. He nips at me playfully before releasing me from his hold. "Oh," I say as an afterthought. "I may or may not have found someone. He's with two of my beasts."

Demon raises an eyebrow at me. "Found someone?"

I roll my eyes, "Look, Cornelius was a piece of shit. He had a young shifter there, locked up in this gross room. The kid is scared. He needs help."

Demon softens and nods. "Okay. We can help him."

I snap my fingers, Lark and Cora herding Ari into the club house. His eyes are huge as they search the space. "Ari, this is my mate Demon. Demon, this is Ari." Demon's eyes widen in understanding the moment he sees the state of the boy. If possible, the kid looks even worse in the light of the bar; deep bruises shine under his eyes, the unruly hair greasy and his too thin frame barely keeping the shirt on.

"Dios," he says gruffly.

"I got you, Pres," the Latin man says, moving with care to

the boy. "Come on, *pequeño lobo*." Ari looks wide eyed at me, hesitant to go with Dios.

"Lark and Cora will go with you." He seems to relax at my words and settles, allowing Dios to herd him back outside.

Stepping back I cock my head to the side, raking my eyes over this new body I get to explore. His freckled face, long hair, clean beard, and tattoos over his large muscular frame make me swoon. "You look different." He raises his eyebrows and I laugh. "A good different."

"So do you," he says. My heart softens; the overwhelming feeling of relief that I'm suddenly standing in front of him washes over me like a tidal wave. Tears that I haven't allowed to fall for so long start to finally break free, and when a small whimper escapes me, Demon sweeps me up into his arms. His scent invades me as I cry into his leather vest. He smells like *home*.

Demon

Survival for people like us is often at the cost of our humanity. We trade soft moments for brutal truths and vulnerability isn't something in our vocabulary. People like us have learned the hard way what it means to trust the wrong people. So, as tears swim in her eyes and I watch her facade crack open, I can't help but marvel at her undying trust in me. I wrap my arms around her body, breathing in her scent and letting out a long groan as I drag her mouth to mine.

My lips are met with a saltwater exorcism.

"I missed you so much," she cries when she pulls away from me. "I wish I had died with you; so many times I begged the gods. Begged them to take me. To release me from this purgatory."

My heart beats erratically, and my stomach becomes

queasy. Pressing my forehead to hers, I breathe her in again. "You found me. We have each other again. No one is ever going to separate us again. Do you hear me? I will kill every single witch, vampire, and shifter who tries to take you from me again."

It's a declaration and a promise that's sealed with a savage kiss. I claim her mouth, the world around us fading away until it's only her lips and body that matter. She climbs me, her legs wrapping around my waist as I palm her full ass and kiss down her neck.

Slamming her on the pool table, primal need has my hands ripping at her pants as she manages to shuck her jacket off. I'm greeted with red lace panties, the crotch darkened with wetness. I growl as she pulls down her tank top, her tits popping out to expose her dark nipples standing erect in the bar light. When my mouth sucks one in, my tongue exploring her, I'm rewarded with a long, loud whimper from her.

"How wet will you be when I touch you?" I ask between sucking on her nipples. My fingers meander down to the apex of her thighs, creating a slow, tortuous pattern before I finally rub across those lace panties. She pushes up against the light pressure, her body shaking.

"You want me?" I chuckle out.

A frustrated growl emanates from her lush lips. My tongue swirls her nipple again, the taste electrifying my body and zapping my patience. My fingers slip under the band and press into her heat.

"FUCK!" she screams. The sound is a symphony to my ears. My own growl adds to the sounds as I pump a few more times, her hips bucking with me before I stop and pull away. I slip my fingers from her tight channel, licking them clean before shucking off the leather cut and unbuttoning my pants. My length springs free, and the Prince Albert piercing glints in the bar lighting.

"That looks fun," she says, eyes wide and locked on the piece of shining metal.

"Being a wolf has given me a few upgrades," I smirk at her as I draw her attention to my knot, my fist bumping into it as I grip my length., "This is going to be fast and hard, *mo chreach bheag.*"

She rips her lace panties before spreading her legs wide. Even decades apart and in a different body her scent remains the same. Her arousal perfumes the air around me, causing my eyes to roll back in my head and forcing my hand to grip the base of my cock hard so I don't lose it.

(RIP- Neoni)

"Do your worst, *Deamhan.* Make it hurt." Hearing my old nickname on her tongue snaps the minimal restraint I was trying to keep.

"Suck it," I demand, dragging her body off the table. Her warm mouth envelopes the smooth head of my cock and her tongue laps at the precum bubbling from my slit. She swallows me down quickly, taking me almost to the root before I feel her gag. When she moves to pull back I fist her hair, keeping her in place. "You breathe when I tell you to breathe," I growl.

Sweet pain pricks my thighs from her claws digging into my flesh. Warmth runs down my thighs and the scent of blood mixes with the arousal in the air. My balls tighten up at the feeling of the pain she is causing with her nails and the pleasure she is pulling from me with her sinful mouth.

The sight of her on her knees, white hair fisted in my hand, sends me into a fury of desire. Pulling my cock from the warm home of her mouth, spit trailing behind, I throw her back onto the table. A few fist pumps and I'm releasing on her wet pussy, my cum coating her.

"Oh, fuck. That's so hot," she moans out as one last splash lands on her.

I smirk, rubbing it into her, demanding she is covered in my scent. Starting at her clit, I work it down and push some into her wet cunt. She cries out, her back arching up off the pool table. The muscles of her pussy clench around my thick fingers.

"You are going to feel so fucking good with my cock shoved into that tight cunt." I thrust into her, curling in a come-hither motion before retreating.

A savage growl rips from her throat. "Stop messing with me and fuck me." She loops her legs around me, digging her heels in to drag me closer.

Lining up the tip of my cock, I lock eyes with her. "Keep those open, I want to see the look on your face when you take every inch of me." Slowly I push the head in, the glint of the piercing disappearing into the heavenly space waiting to squeeze the life from me.

Sliding into her feels like a reckoning. She lets out a long moan, those sharpened nails now sliding down my bare back and sending shivers through my entire being. I watch my cock disappear into her before pulling it back out slowly, repeating the process again and again until I'm soaked and met with no resistance. Her body writhes under me, as breathy pleas to move faster pour from her lips.

"Fuckkk, you take me so good. Look at that tight cunt. My little whore."

She pauses only for a moment, her hand gripping my throat in a quick move. "*Don't* call me that." Power flashes through those green eyes, red magic ringing the iris. My wolf meets her, my eyes glowing brilliant blue. Something in me goes feral at the idea of why she doesn't like being called that, my wolf ready to rip apart the city in search of whoever hurt my mate.

"You are *my* whore. No one else's. And this tight cunt will take my cock and all the cum I can push into you so no one questions who you belong to. Because your body belongs to me." *Thrust.* "Your heart belongs to me." *Thrust.* "This tight cunt belongs to me." *Thrust.*

Her hand falls away from my throat, the magic retreating as she is drawn back into our moment. Those gorgeous eyes roll back in her head as I stroke her clit.

"And this orgasm?" Her pussy trembles around me. "That fucking belongs to me." I bite down hard on the apex of her neck laying my claiming mark, my wolf refusing to allow her to walk away without it.

"Oh fuck, oh fuck," she cries, her pussy starting to convulse around me. "I'm going to cum. I'm going to cum!" I unleash myself at the feel of her letting go, pounding into her as I chase my own release. My knot aches to be inside her, the pain almost unbearable.

She's still riding the waves of her orgasm when I pull off her neck, licking the leftover blood from the wound before pushing up. I keep her pinned with my hand. My release is like a tidal wave through my body; everything empties into her until I let myself collapse down on her naked body.

Our ragged breathing is the only sound in the bar aside from the distant rumble of thunder.

My cock slips from her, bringing out combined releases with it. I slowly push up, spreading her legs even wider so I can see the mess we made. It has my dick twitching. "Gods, that is fucking hot."

She looks utterly spent, a slight rose color spreading across the milky skin of her cheeks. She smiles at me and for a moment I can see our old life flash before us. We had nothing but each other, barely making ends meet and it was worth it.

"Why didn't you knot me?" she asks, breaking the silence.

Leaning down I plant a soft kiss to her abused lips. "Because when I knot you, it'll be when we are fully mated again. Not in this shit hole bar where anyone could walk in on us." She smiles softly at me, nodding in understanding.

"You're just as beautiful in this life as you were in the other, Kallen. So fucking beautiful."

She pushes up and cocks her eyebrow at me, placing her hand on my face. "You look good to me, my love, my *Deamhan*. I think I like you as a shifter." When she begins to close her legs, I let out a growl.

I drop down between her open legs, needing to pray before the goddess spread out in front of me. "I need to worship you, I want to taste us." It's the only warning I give before my tongue is plunging into her. Our combined taste is better than any damn meal I could get.

She cries out as I fuck her oversensitive pussy with my tongue, before I move upward and pay homage to the most important part of her anatomy. My mouth circles her clit, sucking the tiny bud of nerves in before lavishing it with my tongue. It doesn't take long before she's cuming on my face in a breathy moan.

When I ring the last of the pleasure from her I push up onto my knees, grabbing onto her and dragging her onto the bar floor. Her naked body lands directly on top of mine.

"Fuck, you have a talented tongue... so glad you know where the clit is," she moans, snuggling into my chest,

I laugh. "You think I'm just going to shove my tongue in and shake my head around? I'm not an amateur."

"Demon," she murmurs. I can feel the moment slipping by, the closeness we had turning into a chasm between us. "We need to talk."

"I just got you back; it hasn't even been an hour and you want to talk? With my cum dripping down those fine legs?" I hate the distance she's forcing between us. "We've spent lifetimes apart, Kallen, I don't want to fucking talk. I want to hold my mate and enjoy you." I hug her tighter to my naked body. "Don't fucking push me away. Not when we just found each other again."

Kallen

Hearing Demon beg me in his way breaks my heart. Because he's right; we just found each other and something about the reunion scares me more than I thought it would. Feeling him on top of me reminded me of just how long we were apart and all the things that happened in between. I don't regret any of the actions that led me here, but I'm over-whelmed with the sadness of everything we missed out on.

Nothing about this is easy. I may have come home but the house has been rebuilt, with only a few items of our original life.

"Should I have asked about cumming inside you?" His voice pulls me from my thoughts, but I keep my head on his chest. The question catches me off guard for a moment until my memories are unlocked from our old life.

At one point we wanted kids. A family of our own to make up for the mistakes of the ones who raised us.

I shake my head. "You have nothing to worry about. I can't have children." Reem had been sad about it; she had wanted her own family until she realized what kind of people the original families were. Until I showed her the truth.

"I'm sorry, *mo chreach bheag*. I know you wanted children."

"I've made peace with how my life is. I'm done mourning everything they took from me," I shrug. For a moment I consider telling him what I lost, what *we* lost. But I keep that secret locked away; that grief shoved in the dark recesses of my mind to protect him.

"From us," he says. "They took from us."

Emotions threaten to overtake me and just as I'm about to get dragged under, Laoch materializes out of the corner with a soft snort. A reminder of what needs to be said, what needs to be done. Taking a deep breath I shove it all down once again, vowing to deal with it another time.

"Like I said. We need to talk." He crosses his arms over his chest, eyebrow raising. He stares me down, eyes tracing over my body in a hungry yet lazy way. "I know what you're doing."

"What am I doing?" he chuckles.

"Distracting me," I say, shoving his shirt at him as I get dressed again. He doesn't deny it but he does slip the shirt and jeans back on.

"Alright, what's so important that you forced us to get dressed after being separated for so long?"

Anxiety is a foreign emotion for me. Anger, rage, grief? Those I'm well acquainted with. But anxiety is new, and as I stand in front of my mate, about to tell him what we are up against, I hate that my chest feels tight and my stomach rolls uncomfortably.

Noticing my shift, Demon steps forward and takes my face in his hands. "Hey, whatever you have to say, it'll be okay."

I take a deep breath, allowing his sea salt and cedar scent to bath me. His eyes search my face for any clue on how to support me. This is the Demon I remember, the one who could read my mood without a word and supported me without thought. So I take another deep breath, steading my heart and telling the anxiety to fuck off.

"I was given a vision. . ."

FOUR

This new body is stronger. The witch, Phylis, was able to push against me. I changed my mind after the last faded away. I wanted help, to see if the souls could be an ally in this fucked up scenario. But sadly she had no interest in it, and her soul met the same fate as the first two. I can't help but thank her though; using her elemental magic to burn those fools alive was satisfying.
-Personal Journal of Kallen

Kallen

The cool night air of Gothic Grove pushes through my hair as we turn the corner on his bike into the clubhouse parking lot. Gothic Grove has two seasons, shit and shittier. Tonight the weather has taken a turn, and it won't be long until snow blankets the ground and solstice is upon us.

Fuck, how long has it been since I celebrated solstice? Since I cele-brated any holiday?

A flash of Samhain pushes up briefly; Astrea and Ava fighting Cordelia, the feel of Kara holding me hostage. A shiver runs down my spine involuntarily. Telling Demon even part of what was coming had brought up the past in a swift and ruthless way, reminding me what I had to lose.

Demon's black Harley Davidson rumbles between my legs, dragging me away from that night. Various other bikes are parked in a straight line outside the building; lights filling the gravel lot, so no area is shadowed. The pulse of music can be heard coming from inside along with laughter. The large structure looks like a concrete warehouse, with a neon sign above it flashing Primal Knights MC. The chain-link fence bordering the property has me feeling uneasy, the urge to rip it apart strong.

Demon pulls the bike to a stop, allowing me to unwrap myself and dismount. His body is rigid as he scans the lot for any danger. The news I delivered stole the carefree energy he had prior. Not having the mating bond complete was a risky move as well, adding to his tension.

A half-completed bond is dangerous for a wolf; they tend to grow violent with any perceived threat to their mate. If I was smart or cared more for the pack, I would have pushed to complete it. My blood lust isn't something I care to keep in check and the thought of fucking my mate in the blood of a fresh kill is far too tempting to pass up. Fucked up? Sure. But I was painted as the villain the moment I became powerful.

He turns his blue gaze back to me, body finally relaxing. *"Mo chreach bheag,* I don't want my pack smelling you like this. I'll have to kill them all." He pulls me close and nuzzles into my neck. The old language on his tongue sounds divine and makes me want that tongue between my thighs again.

I laugh, "This life has made you jealous."

A somber look moves over his face. "I've spent lifetimes living alone, living with the knowledge that I lost you. That I failed you."

Guilt assaults me, another new emotion. I had known something was wrong, all those years ago. But I had let him leave our home anyway, let him meet Arthor Mori. I've never forgiven myself, the guilt still cutting off my supply of air. Demanding I pay with my life for the mistake I made. "*Deamhan*, I need to tell you something." The words sit on my tongue, the confession that needs to happen, but I choke on them, a sob coming out instead.

Gods damn it, he deserves to know the truth. Get it together!

My internal battle rages as tears spill over. Demon pulls me into his body tenderly. "It's okay, Kallen." My frame shakes as I'm racked with all the regret, and guilt, and fear, and anger. All the emotions that are threatening to drown me. "Breathe, *mo chreach bheag.*"

My voice cracks. "I. . . I knew something was wrong. I should have told you. I should have listened to my instincts." The words tumble out and take on a life of their own as we stand under the floodlights in the gravel parking lot. I keep muttering 'I'm sorry' over and over, a broken prayer leaving my lips in an act of confession. He says nothing, only keeps me pressed to his body. I pull back, dropping to my knees in front of him, head bowed in submission. "I do not deserve it but I'll beg anyway. Please, *please,* forgive me."

It feels like an eternity that I'm on my knees, looking at the cracked pebbles that my knees are pressed into, before he hauls me up. "Never get on your knees before me unless you are choking on my dick. Do you understand?" His tone is commanding, leaving no room for argument. I nod quickly. "The witches are the ones that should apologize; they took us from each other. Not you." Tension leaves my body in a wave as soon as I hear those words and I sink back into his embrace.

He shakes, as if his own ocean of emotions is threatening to pull him under.

"I made them pay," I whisper. "I made them suffer."

But it was never enough.

Demon looks at me, cupping my face between his hands as if he knows my inner thoughts. "It *is* enough because it brought you back to me." He plants a tender kiss on my forehead. "Now let me remind you who you belong to."

Kallen

The morning light filters through the cracked blinds of Demon's bedroom. We spent the night fucking in every position, and my body has the bruises to prove it. The mating bond, however, is still incomplete. The disappointment had been visceral when I realized he had no intention of doing it. The insidious question of why we didn't complete it kept me up most the night, long after he passed out.

I fucking hate anxiety; why is this a thing?

I scoot my naked body to the edge of the bed before letting my bare feet touch down on the old brown carpet. Demon's room at the clubhouse is small but well put together. His full-size bed takes up most of the space with a chest of drawers pushed up against the right side of the wall. A small desk occupies the other wall, and his leather cut hangs over the chair pushed into it. My moans had filled the room right alongside his as we found solace in each others' arms. The echoing pleasure drowned out the noise from the party raging outside the door.

(Your love feat. Roniit- One True God)

Padding my way towards the bathroom, I flick on the light, illuminating the tiled shower. I groan at the sight; despite it being small, it looks like pure heaven. Steam billows out as I turn the water as hot as it'll go. Stepping in, the moan that erupts from my mouth is sinful as the hot water cascades down me, soothing my sore muscles. Closing my eyes I lose myself in the feel of it all, breathing in the salt water and pine scent that seems to envelope me. Strong hands startle me as they circle my body; those tattooed fingers that pulled endless pleasure from me last night dip down the curve of my stomach, landing against my pussy..

"Mmmm…all wet for me?" he murmurs as he licks the claiming mark. My knees weaken for a moment as the feeling shoots straight to my clit. He chuckles while his fingers delicately stroke my wet center, the touch feather-light and driving me crazy. Every pass he makes increases the heat spreading through my body, while also growing my frustration.

"Fuckkkkkk," I groan, not bothering to hide my emotions.

My wolf spins me around, shoving my body against the cool tile wall by my throat. He squeezes hard, my breath barely making its way to my lungs now. The feeling electrifies my body, a current moving through my veins that is unstoppable. My magic rises up, alive with curiosity and pulses around us.

His grip tightens and my eyes roll back in my head, the feeling divine. The thought of how much power he holds right now has my pussy flooding. Every part of my body tingles in anticipation of his next move. He pulls me off the wall again, slowly turning us so he is leaning against the wall, and pushes my knees to the shower floor. His pierced cock now in my line of sight.

"I need your lips wrapped around my cock, *mo chreach bheag*, like the good little whore you are." He lets out a low growl that vibrates every bone in my body as I take him into my mouth. "You look so beautiful like this, on your knees." He pumps again and again until the speed is relentless and I'm gagging, barely hanging on to reality. Tears stream down my face but are lost in the water cascading down from the shower head. It's as though I could drown at any moment, and that simple brush with death feels better than any drug.

Pulling from my mouth in a fast move, I feel the hot spray of his release across my chest and my mouth, his voice a rough shout as it happens. My eyes watch his massive body coil and relax as the last of his essence drops onto me. His stomach muscles are tight, covered in tattoos, and his hands push through his red hair as he refocuses on me still on my knees. His cock is still hard and at the ready, that extra bump of flesh at the base engorged.

"Look at you covered in me." His smile is wicked across his handsome face. "No one will question who you belong to."

My chest hurts for a moment and the words tumble from me like an avalanche. "So why won't you complete the bond?"

He drags me to a stand, leaning in. "I wanted to make it special. Lord knows the first time we did it wasn't, but it seems my mate is impatient." His mouth is hot on the bite he left, and it is the only warning I get. His teeth slide into the sensitive skin, into the claiming mark he already started.

Demon

(Unholy- Kayla King)

Kallen's blood floods my mouth the same way her screams of pleasure fill the small bathroom. My wolf loves the idea that the whole club house will hear her screams, smell her arousal. I move us out of the shower, my teeth still latched into her neck as my wolf rubs against her dark magic. A red haze forming over my eyes as her magic fills my whole body; that intoxicating, dark magic.

"Please," she whimpers as I drop her wet body onto my small bed. "Fucking hell *Deahmon,* please, please." The sound of her begging gets sweeter and sweeter the more I hear it.

Pulling off her ravaged neck, blood dripping down my chin, I lean into her ear. "I'm going to let my knot stretch you to your limit. I'm going to keep pumping you full of my cum. I want to breed you, *mo chreach bheag.*"

"Oh, fuck yes. I want to feel it, I want you dripping out of me all day." The dirty words pouring from her snap any control I was pretending to have. Notching the head of my cock against her wet entrance, I push in with one stroke. Her hands squeeze both breasts hard, nails digging into that soft skin. Her head is thrown back in a silent scream as her back arches off the bed.

"Move!" she pants. "I need to feel you move!" Tears prick the corner of her eyes, emotions cresting over her again and again.

My hips jerk forward as I start rutting her into the bed, our mating bond continuing to form within us again. I'm lost to the sensation as the magic binds us together again. The rightness of this all threatens to break me apart. When I claim her mouth, she bites down hard on my lip, the taste of iron blending with her own spicy flavor. The kiss takes no prisoners, our bodies telling the story of lifetimes apart.

"You feel so good," she groans, pulling back slightly. "I need you, I need you to fill me." Her words break apart as she sobs and begs.

My world begins and ends with her – who am I to deny this? "Touch yourself...make yourself cum all over my dick before I knot you." She whimpers, her hand finding her clit. She strokes herself expertly and it only takes a moment before she comes apart, her pussy starting to convulse and squeeze my cock.

My knot begins to swell at the base, and slowly I push in as the tissue enlarges. She tenses; even as her orgasm continues to crest, she winces at the intrusion. "Shh, relax, *mo chreach bheag.* Let me in." I snake my hand down, catching her fingers as I help continue to draw circles around her clit. Slowly she relaxes under me, her body yielding to the knot. "That's a good girl. So good with your greedy pussy. You take it all so well." One last shove and I'm fully seated, the flesh locking us together.

My cum shoots out, painting her and filling her to the brim. The feeling sends me into a frenzy as I rock my hips to gain friction.

"Oh gods. Oh yes. Oh, fuck that feels good. Fill me up, please don't stop." She moans over and over. Blood has dripped into her white hair that is spread out around her in a halo. My mouth finds hers again, peppering kisses to her soft lips as our pleasure continues to ravage our bodies; that bond finally settling into the matching empty spaces in our chests.

I'm not sure how long we lay there. Time loses meaning to our pleasure but eventually, my knot decreases enough that I slip from her. My wolf is preening at the amount of our release we left in her. His deep infatuation with filling our mate to the brim makes me want to do it all over again. The happy pulse down the bond from her has me smiling, and the savage claiming mark contrasting her milky skin has me feeling overly satisfied.

Some wolves would have been delicate, but delicate doesn't match us, not anymore. The ripped flesh is a reminder of who we are now.

"Keep looking at me like that and we won't leave this bed for the rest of our lives," she says in a husky voice. Her green eyes have a familiar silver ring around them now, a sign of our bond.

"Would that be so bad?" I ask, pulling her over to me, those sharp black nails playing over my chest. When her hot center settles over my cock I feel our combined release start to seep from her.

Good, I'll wear our scents like a badge of honor.

"No," she sighs. "But we don't have the luxury of it right now. I can't lose you again."

She pulls out of my arms, standing from the bed with her naked body on full display. A deep satisfaction rumbles in me when I watch her pull on ripped shorts without cleaning herself up. Throwing an oversize t-shirt over the black lace bra barely covering her tits, she watches me, enjoying the view of my naked body.

"I don't want anyone seeing you like this," I growl, noting the transparent nature of her t-shirt.

Her face falls into annoyance, "The bar full of shifters out there is going to smell your cum dripping down my thighs." She bends down and crawls across the bed to me, swiping her hair to the side to show her ravaged neck. "And this mark will show them exactly who I belong to. So cut the shit and let's go."

"Jesus," I mutter. She stands back up, pausing for a moment before she pushes her hand down the front of her shorts.

"Fuckkk." The groan is pulled from my lips as I watch her bring those two fingers to her mouth, licking our combined releases off them.

"Mmm. We taste good." She gives me a savage smile before raising her eyebrow and putting her hair up in a messy bun. I know she's doing it to show the mark I've left on her.

When we finally exit the room Dios catches my eye, a smirk moving over his lips. When his nostrils flare I know he smells us. I watch his gaze move to her, no doubt seeing the claiming mark and blood that she refused to wash away,

"Is everyone here?" Kallen asks me. The room is silent but the air feels tense, uncomfortable even. Rucker's sharp glare cuts into me. He has a few wolves near him, all with equal looks of disdain for my mate addressing the room. The pack may follow me, but it's clear Rucker has been hard at work in swaying some towards him.

That is an issue for another day; one thing at a time.

I nod and cross my arms over my chest, leaning back against the wall while she stands facing out to the men around us.

"Hell is coming for Gothic Grove," she says as if she's reading the weather. "And if we don't stop it, they'll slaughter us all."

<hr>

Kallen

You could hear a pin drop in the silence before the one named Rucker lets out a barking laugh. "Hell hasn't invaded in centuries; they have no interest in Gothic Grove."

Shooting him a glare that I hope conveys a painful death if he continues to doubt me, I go on. "You are correct, for the most part. The royal family has no interest. But The Order of Infernal Sin does. They want Hell, and by extension, Gothic Grove."

Blank faces stare back at me. None of them understand the gravity of the situation.

"What of the royal family?" the man who smells of the underworld asks. His strange mismatched blue and green eyes pop brightly against his smooth coco skin. Two metal snake bite piercings gleam on either side of his lip, and his body is covered in tattoos - including his shaved head.

"What of them? As far as I know, the previous king is dead," I say with a straight face. If I'm not mistaken, Dios's eyes flash with alarm for a moment.

"So? Why do we care if they take control of Hell?" Rucker asks, forcing me to look away from the Latino man. "So what if this Order decides they want control? That's on the royals to deal with, not us. If they do end up coming here, we'll kill them all. No one fucks with us."

A low growl comes from beside me as one of my Hellbeasts pads up, sitting its massive body to my right. "Spoken like a typical man," I sneer. "Tell me, have you ever watched an Elker feast on someone's soul while they drown in nightmares?" Wolves shift uncomfortably as I look around the room. "Or seen what Hell's magic can do to someone like you?"

I glare at Rucker. "Men like those in The Order only want one thing. Power. They've already eliminated the previous king. They are going after the prince now."

Still, no one says anything. A few members clear their throats awkwardly. Looking around the room I catch Dios watching me, his face taking a pale hue to it.

"This is a load of bullshit." I shift my eyes back to Rucker as he complains. "Demon, tell me you don't believe this shit."

I don't have to turn around to see Demon's reaction – it seeps down the bond. Smooth and slow like honey, it settles any doubt I could have that he would side with his club. "She's my mate. I would believe her without question, Rucker."

His face flushes and his eyes narrow as he sends every ounce of loathing he has for me into that look. I can see the wheels spinning – he's trying to figure out how to discredit me. The argument is on the tip of his tongue that I'm not who I say I am.

My mismatched eye friend steps forward. "She's his *alma gemela*. Soul mate. Can't you see that?" He tilts his head to the side, the sensation of my soul being gazed upon running through my blood. "Her soul is old, older than any of us."

"What are you?" I ask, my brows drawn low in confusion.

He shrugs. *"El dador de la Muerte."*

"I didn't ask who you *were*, Giver of Death, I asked *what* you are."

Before he can say anything, Demon steps forward. "Dios is

my sergeant-at-arms. We'll leave it at that." I try not to let my annoyance in his tone melt down the bond. He looks out over the pack. "If Kallen says there is a threat to us, we believe her. If you want to disagree with that you can leave." He directs the last part to Rucker, regardless that he wears the VP patch.

Rucker, unable to stop his mouth from moving, shifts the topic. "Are we going to talk about how she killed Lainey? I've been trying to get a hold of Cornelious all day. He's not answering."

My eyes narrow at him, disliking that he has close contact with the man I killed. "Careful, Rucker. I took care of him and his little circle. Don't make me wonder if I missed a rat during that purge."

"What are you talking about?" he asks, a whiff of fear echoing into my ear.

I glance down at my long nails, playing with my cuticle as I attempt to avoid stabbing the man. "Her pedophile father is dead, those that were loyal to him are dead and any that were willing to be loyal to us are awaiting our command. I'm going to hope for your sake, Rucker, that you had no idea he was trafficking young individuals." Rucker pales, but says nothing. It's enough for me to crave his blood on my hands.

Demon's warm presence moves into me, pulling my body against his. "Dios, go follow up with that. I want to know everything that he was involved in and who was helping him. The rest of you — we go to Church."

FIVE

Kallen

Despite all the things Demon has done for me, all the rules he's broken for me, people he's killed, his refusal to allow me into Church annoys the fuck out of me.

"It's club members only, and no women," he had said, kissing me on the forehead.

Rucker looked pleased. It made me want to slit his throat. Daydreams of how his warm blood would coat my hands play through my mind.

I look back at the door behind me, rolling my eyes as I sip on the beer. The clock is ticking; we cannot continue to debate.

If this doesn't end, I'm going to Drago and Shadow. I need someone to help and if the club won't, the dragons will. They have a vested interest in this.

"You look annoyed." Dios smooth voice pulls me from my thoughts as he slides up to the bar. While the bond tells me Demon is still busy, I can't help but feel disappointed.

I glance over at him. "I *am* annoyed. We are wasting time." I pull the pocket knife from my book, edging the blade in the old wooden bar.

The old bartender slides two shot glasses down and leaves a fifth of tequila next to us before making himself scarce. Dios pours the clear liquid, passing one to me before sliding the other shot glass to himself. Narrowing my eyes at the offending substances, I contemplate if it really should be a tequila drinking night.

Dios snorts, "*Te ves nervisoa.* You look nervous."

"Of course I'm nervous, I am as close to a basic bitch as one can get. Which means undoubtedly if I drink too much of this, I'll end up topless on this bar." I pause for a moment. "Or I'll end up gutting Rucker. Honestly, it's fifty-fifty." Reaching over the bar, I grab a small lime before shooting the liquid down. Dios arches an eyebrow at me as I bite and suck the lime. "What? I said I was nervous. Not that I wouldn't do it."

He chuckles as he pours himself another shot. "You know something you aren't sharing." he muses, keeping his eyes forward and slowly sipping his drink.

Shrugging, I take another shot.

"A few years back, we brought a newbie in and ended up trusting him too quickly. It cost the club a lot of good wolves by the time he was done with us. Including Rucker's sister." Turning to look at me, he passes another shot my way. "You are Demon's mate, but this is his pack; you need to show your loyalty to them. Show them you have the pack's best interest at heart."

I'm quiet for a long while; so long, in fact, that Dios pushes away from the bar. "Dios, I will do everything in my power to keep my mate with me. Even if that means going against this fucking pack. You would do well to remember that."

He doesn't say anything, but he does pause to contemplate my words.

Shaking my head, I continue, "If the pack won't help me, I have two dragons who will."

Dios freezes at the mention of the dragons. Recognition flashes across his strained expression. "If you care for Demon, you won't use that option," he snarls, venom dripping from his voice.

My eyes narrow. "I'll do what I have to."

He leans in close, violence radiating off him. "And if you bring the attention of them to us, I will kill you myself to protect him."

I hold his gaze, never flinching, letting him see he can try to kill me all he wants but he won't win. "Do you have a history with them?"

"His father had a history with them—a bloody history. Stay the fuck out of it." he growls at me before pushing away and leaving me alone again.

I let out a long breath. While I was serious that I don't care about the pack, I also know there is some truth to what Dios said. It's the only thing that makes me start planning how to solve this quickly. Because like it or not, I am going to need the pack's trust if we have even a slight chance of surviving this.

(Bad Girlfriend- Theory of a Deadman)
When Demon comes out of Church, he finds me on my

third beer with a half empty bottle of tequila next to it, and well and truly on my way to being intoxicated.

He gives me a lopsided grin, those dimples popping out, as I turn and face him. "Hello, *mo chreach bheag*. You look like you are having a good time out here." He nuzzles into my neck, nipping playfully. I let out a long moan at the feel of his lips.

"Fuck, I missed you." I groan, not caring that the bar is full of people. Wrapping my legs around his waist, I claim his mouth with my own. The kiss burns a path straight to my pussy. My hands reach up and bury into his thick hair as I grind myself against him.

He pulls back for a moment. "You keep doing that and I'll fuck you right here in front of my whole club."

"You say that like it's a bad thing." I nip at his bottom lip. My right hand snakes down to his impressive length straining against his tight jeans. "I think you like the idea of that, of showing who this pussy belongs to. Of showing them just what I look like when I come apart on you."

He growls low at me, the sound vibrating my core, as I stroke him over his jeans. "Keep talking and I'll stuff that mouth so full of my cock you'll be choking on me."

"Promises, promises," I tsk before he slams his mouth into mine again. His hands are swift as they grapple with my breasts through my shirt.

"You going to share her?" A crude voice interrupts the moment. A younger wolf stares at us with a hungry expression. His polo with the collar flipped up and designer jeans make him stand out against the room full of leather. "I'd fuck you so hard I'd be in your womb, baby."

Demon grumbles low, a warning growl, but I push him away from me, standing to my full height. "I'm sorry... did you just say you'd fuck into my womb?" He smirks, thinking this is somehow a turn on. "Bro, I hate to tell you this but no one wants to be fucked to the womb. My cunt literally dried up while you were talking. That's female pleasure 101. Did you sleep through that class? Or were you too busy putting white powder up your nose while your buddies did keg stands?"

His face turns red, flushed with embarrassment. A few chuckles spread through the bar before I hear people agreeing with me. Dios swings his arm over the wannabe frat boy's shoulders. "Come on, *joder chico,* let me give you a lesson in female anatomy and pleasure." He looks like he wants to argue, but Dios pulls him closer. "That wasn't a request. Either come with me, or Kallen rips your dick off and feeds it to her little pack of *perros malvados.*"

Dios drags the man off, even as my beasts plan to meet them outside. I smile at the fear that will no doubt fill the fuck boy.

The music shifts, the rock beat taking me away and making my hips move. The tequila makes me think dancing on the bar is a good idea. Demon realizes my plan a moment too late as I vault up onto the old bar. Cheers push me forward as I lose myself to the music, my hands running up and down my body and into my hair.

I keep my eyes trained on my mate as he crosses his arms over his chest, an amused look splaying over his face now. As I start to hike my shirt up, he raises his eyebrow at me. "Careful," he growls.

"Or what?" I laugh over the music.

Walking up, he wraps a hand around my ankle, dragging me forward. My balance shifts and I land with a huff over his shoulder, his hand planting firmly on my ass in a loud smack. The wolves around us laugh more before going back to their own drinks and groups.

"You enjoy taunting me?" he growls as he lets me slide down his body.

I land a kiss on his lips, my tongue tracing over him before plunging into his mouth. He groans and leans into the kiss, hands traveling up and down before gripping my ass hard.

"I want to take you back to our room and fuck you senseless," he moans, pulling back.

A ripple of power moves through the room, making me push back away from Demon. My eyes scan the room for the source, the hairs on my arms and neck prickling and sending a warning of danger. From the shadows my Hellbeasts emerge, as if they too feel a shift. I notice it only seconds before Demon does.

"Oh shit, incoming!" I scream. The room erupts in shadows and crackling lighting. Screams pierce the air as people run for cover. My Hellbeasts arrive at my side, blending into the thick shadows as if they are one. When another crack of lighting shows through, I watch a blond winged man drop into the bar covered in blood and gore, a large sword clattering out of his hand as he braces himself on the dirty floor. The moment he hits the ground the shadows disappear, as if sucked into the large black wings protruding at an odd angle from his muscular back. As if something grabbed hold of one and cracked it down the middle.

He stands swiftly, swaying on his feet, grabbing the discarded sword only to heft it upward and slice through a giant creature that appears just behind him via an open portal. A shower of blood coats the man, awakening my own lust for violence. Dios shoots forward, grabbing the second creature that appears just behind it, ripping it into two with his bare hands

"Close the fucking portal!" Dios shouts at him as another pushes through. The streets of Hell are just beyond, screams and snarls and ripping sounds pulsing into the room. It's evident wherever he is coming from is not a place we want to have open to the bar.

The newcomer freezes, exhaustion pulling at him as his eyes meet mine. Silver eyes.

"And this is why you should never have men in charge," I mutter. Demon's body blocks mine, my hands pushing him to the side so I can move forward. Releasing my own Realm Walker magic I knit the portal close, feeling a familiarity as I brush against the man's magic.

Dusting off my hands I look around. The pieces of the creatures are smoldering, their remains slowly turning to ash until they are only a puff of smoke.``Stand down, little king," I say. "Nothing will be getting through." The newcomer remains tense, but allows his sword to drop, the tip of the blade hitting the floor.

His eyes widen a fraction as if he is just now realizing where he is. As if he didn't mean to come here. "How do you know who I am?"

I cross my arms, smiling at him."Your little sister looks just like you. Did you know that?"

He frowns. "Ava? You've seen Ava? Where is she?" His eyes sweep the room with frantic energy before they land on Dios. "*You.*"

The waiver in his voice has me ready to move, to catch him. Dios, however, beats me to it and catches the man as he slumps towards the ground.

"*Mi cielo.*" Dios says, a sense of awe in his voice.

Ava's brother doesn't say anything, eyes rolling in the back of his head before he passes out.

Demon

Chaos erupted the moment Dios had caught the man. Through the bond I could feel Kallen's unease, an emotion I hated coming from her. It makes my skin crawl. In response, my wolf demanded I take her someplace safe.

My home is one of the few still standing in the area looking out over the port, the sea breeze allowing the salty smell to waft up through the old windows. The chipped white paint across the porch and frame show the years of weathering and beatings the home has taken with each coastal storm that assaults it. Nerves make me pause, my neck burning with embarrassment as I look over at Kallen.

Her eyes swim with emotion. "You made our dream home," she whispers.

I nod, not trusting myself to speak. Emotions threaten to spill over as I'm assaulted with the memories of late nights planning our escape from this city. Early mornings spent on the beach, barefoot races in the sand, and love-making under the starry sky. Grabbing her hand, I pull us up the porch and into the house.

"I love it." She plants a delicate kiss on my mouth. "Thank you, my *Deahmon.*" I watch her begin to explore, her hands tracing and touching everything. The silver ring in her eyes shines as she searches, for what I don't know. Through the bond I can feel the surge of emotions coming from her.

The shiplapped entrance to my home holds a warm hallway lined with benches for people to place their shoes under. An old chandelier hangs from the vaulted wood-paneled ceiling, casting a glow down. Dios moves past us to the right, up the narrow stairway that leads to the attic bedroom he claimed as his own, the man still cradled in his arms like he could break at any moment.

"Where is he going?" Kallen asks as she slips her shoes off. As she moves towards the kitchen, she pauses. As if on instinct, I watch her trace the spellwork etched into the door frame leading into the kitchen. Spellwork I had tried to replicate from our old home. A memory floods forward of her carving those; a blessing she had called them, and every day she retraced them with her fingers.

"He has a room in the attic," I explain. "Only he and I are keyed to get into this place, no one else can enter uninvited."

Kallen moves off to my left and continues to explore the home as I grab a beer from the fridge. The kitchen is the most up-to-date part of the house. While I don't cook, Dios' love language is feeding people. The white upper cabinets are broken apart by flecked marble countertops before black cabinets line the bottom. Stainless steel appliances are scattered throughout the kitchen.

"What's the deal with you two?" Her voice doesn't hold jealousy, just curiosity. She meanders into the living space, the wall cutting off my view.

I run my hand through my thick auburn hair before drinking down the cool beverage. "We are close, we have shared in the past. If that's what you want to know."

Kallen moves into view again, her body crowding me as her arms loop around my waist. Her cinnamon scent invades every pore of my body. The kiss I plant on her soft lips earns me a long moan. She presses into me harder, demanding more from the kiss. Setting the beer down I grip her thighs hard, lifting her onto the countertop next to us.

"You smell like fucking heaven." I groan as I nip playfully at her neck. My hands reach up and cup her breasts, squeezing hard. "Have you been walking around without a bra on?" Her nipples perk up through the t-shirt as I continue to grope her. She only smiles wickedly. I twist her nipple harder, earning a small yip from her before I shove her shirt up, soothing her with my tongue. We've always been this way, a push-and-pull of pleasure and pain. Even before we became what we are now, we rode the edge during sex.

I continue to lick and bite at her nipple while my hand tugs on the other one. Her hips move, pressing her hot core into my hard dick. Those milky thighs wrap around me, holding me to her. "I need you," she pants.

Unable to deny her, I step back and pull my shirt off quickly. Her eyes rake down my body, taking in the hard muscles I've had cut into me after long hours working out. She sucks in her lower lip, teeth biting down on it as she watches my hands unbutton my jeans and push them down. I grip my cock hard, pumping it into my hand all while her eyes track mine. I raise my eyebrow in a silent gesture.

(Cola- Lana Del Rey)

She doesn't hesitate, dropping to her knees and swallowing me up. "Good girl," I groan as she sucks and swirls her tongue. I'm lost in the sensation as I set the pace, fucking her mouth relentlessly. Her nails dig into my flesh, teeth occasionally applying light pressure to my cock. I'm so lost in the feeling I don't hear Dios come in, but his scent wafts through the small space. Pulling my eyes from the goddess at my feet, I lock eyes with him standing in the doorway. I smile, looking back down and fucking Kallen's face again, gripping her hair roughly. "Oh, fuck I'm right there. Keep going," I groan, the idea of Dios watching us pushing me over the edge as I send my release down the back of her throat. She sucks down every last drop until I'm oversensitive and let out a hiss, forcing her back up.

"Dios," she purrs. "I never would have pegged you for having a voyeurism kink." Her eyes catching his, unconcerned that he's watching us. I lean back onto the counter, cock still jutting out from my body. Kallen pushes up to a stand and drops her panties,exposing her pussy to the room. Her scent perfumes around us.

He crosses his arms over his chest and raises his eyebrow. "You don't know much about me yet."

"Do you want to join us?" I ask as I pull Kallen back against me, my fingers slowly descending until I'm spreading her pussy wide, her arousal dripping from her.

Kallen lets out a long moan, and the temptress spreads her legs a little wider. "Yes," she says. "Come play with us."

Kallen

Dios zeros in on Demon's fingers as he plays with my cunt. Hunger and need blazes in his green and blue irises. He pulls in those lip piercings, one after another before allowing them to pop free, all the while those eyes devouring my body.

"Do you like having him watch?" Demon asks, his voice husky. "Do you like knowing his cock is getting harder and harder watching us? That he'll have to fuck his hand when we are done here." More arousal floods me, my pussy making obscene noises in the quiet kitchen. Demon chuckles. "Yeah, I think you do like it."

I'm lost in the sensations as he circles my clit and those thick digits into me, his tongue licking that brutal claiming mark on my neck. Nothing else matters aside from the pleasure he is giving me and the sensation of him.My eyes flutter shut as my head rests on his shoulder, my lips parting and releasing a moan.

"Open your eyes...look at what you're doing to him," Demon demands.

Unable to deny him, my eyes flutter open. The sight of Dios fisting his thick cock, roughly pumping it up and down, has me coming undone. Screaming, my release flows from me.

My orgasm hits in waves, a never ending crescendo of lust. Demon doesn't allow me a moment to come down from it before he flattens me out on the kitchen table. My breasts are shoved into the hardwood, nipples dragging against it as he kicks my legs wide. His cock notches at my opening, the head barely breaching me in an agonizing tease.

"Demonnnn," I cry - no, beg - as my hips push back, my

desperate need to control every action barreling through my core.

Demon's hot breath hits next to my ear, cedar and sea salt invading my nostrils. "He is going to watch as I fuck my cum deep into you," His slow thrust is fluid; one motion and he's fully inside, my pussy barely able to accommodate his girth. Tears spring forward as I'm overwhelmed with the feeling. When he pulls back and pushes into me again, my cunt quivers and I squeal. Sweat beads on my head while he relentlessly fucks me, the table pushing into my hips hard enough to know I'll have bruises.

I know Dios can see him pushing in and out of me; now he'll be able to watch Demon's cum stream down my leg when he pulls out. Out of the corner of my eye, I can just make out his hand pumping himself at a leisurely pace. His breathing is heavy in the kitchen air.

"You're doing that to him, *mo chreach bheag.* The sight of my cock filling your tight, pink pussy is making him lose control."

I groan, pushing my hips back to meet Demon's thrusts.

"Come over here, Dios," Demon commands. "Baby, help him out with your mouth."

I nod eagerly, my tongue darting out and waiting for the offering of his cock. Dios appears in my line of sight with a smile on his face, pure hunger radiating out from his eyes. His cock, equally as large as Demon's though missing the piercing, is weeping as he slides it past my open lips. The salty taste invades my senses and my thighs clench immediately.

"Oh, fuck, her mouth feels good," Dios chants.

Demon swears, "She looks so good like this. Both holes filled."

"Still has one more to fill," Dios comments. I do my best to display an enthusiastic approval of the idea, and Demon chuckles. It takes a moment before I feel something cool slide down my ass and his thick digit push into me. "Gonna cum," Dios grunts, pulling his cock from me as the spray hits me in the face.

"Oh fuck, Demon, fuck, I'm going to come. Oh fuck!" I'm screaming nonsense as I can feel the orgasm barreling towards me, the feel of Dios's release on me pushing me over. I'm squeezing Demon tightly as he fucks me with a vicious pace, until I can feel him pulsing deep within me. I whimper as he holds me against the hard table. The large bulge of his knot is now pressing into me, the pain sending more wetness down my thighs.

"Look at this good fucking girl, taking my knot so fucking well," Demon moans in my ear as he licks the claiming mark on my neck. I sense Dios coming up next to us, his breath a ghost on my thighs. "I want him to see how I fill you up," Demon says, and I swear to all the gods those words have me cumming again.

SIX

Kallen

(What it Cost- Bad Omens)

Hunting is my new favorite pastime. The feeling of your prey fearing for their life is intoxicating. Particularly when that prey has never known fear. Never known what it means to be weak or vulnerable. My prey tonight knows something is amiss, but he can't put his finger on what. The spot in the shadows where I lurk allows me a full view of his office. Had he understood what it meant to be hunted, he would have glanced at the dark spaces when the lighting cracked overhead, but he didn't. I blink slowly and smile, allowing the two dark snakes to uncoil from my body and drop to the ground.

They move out before me through the muddy yard, the rain beating down around me. My hair is now a curtain in front of my face. The pants and shirt I wear stick to my body, showcasing the knives strapped to me along with my long whip coiled around my torso. I follow my snakes up to the front door, whistling as I go, my dark magic already moving through the home and killing anyone who it contacts.

I refuse to be interrupted.

Standing in front of the two large oak doors that lead into the house, I cock my head and look at the pathetic spell he has etched across the door. I huff out an annoyed laugh as I place my hand flat on the wood. My arm burns momentarily as my magic eats away at the warding, black glittering mist flowing out until the door in front of me dissolves and I step over the threshold. The two black snakes frame me on either side as I continue my quest for the man who helped kill my mate.

"Ohhh Jacob...come out, come out wherever you are," I yell into the quiet house. I continue to whistle as I make my way through the large front entry and move towards the office I know he's hiding in. The scent of magic looms in the air, and if I was an average witch it would have dropped me on my ass. But I'm not an average witch—I'm the fucking Harbinger.

I uncoil the whip from around my torso as I kick open the office door, the balding form of Jacob Cosark hiding behind his desk with his grimoire in front of him. As if the leather bound atrocity will save him from me. He screams as my whip lashes out, slicing his cursed book in half.

"K-K-Kallen..." he stutters. "Please, have mercy." His beady eyes dart around the room but are met with both snakes boxing him.

"Mercy? Don't make me fucking laugh. Did you offer mercy to me? To my fucking mate? No. You only cared about whatever power you could help Arthur gain," I growl.

"You don't understand! We had no choice!" His voice is loud in the quiet room.

Anger burns through me and my power unfurls around me, his eyes going wide. "No choice? You had a fucking choice and you chose greed!" My power grabs him and drags his large body over the desk, dropping him at my feet. The smell of urine makes me roll my eyes.

"You will burn for this. They will not allow you to keep this power! This isn't what Jameson would have wanted, Kallen."

"DON'T YOU SAY HIS FUCKING NAME!" I scream, and my power takes on a mind of its own.

When I come to, I'm covered in pieces of Jacob. The gore coats my skin like armor, my snakes firmly back on my body. And when I leave the house, the forest surrounding it is nothing but a wasteland, my power having killed everything.

I can only smile at the devastation, whistling as I head to the next house.

***

My eyes open to the dark room, my hand automatically grabbing onto Demon for reassurance he is still here. In the inky night, I see the luminous eyes of my Hellbeasts. I let out a shaky breath before draping my body across my mate, Demon nuzzling his face into my neck as he envelopes me in his strong arms. The scent of cedar and ocean wrapping me up, desperately beckoning me back to sleep.

Despite the comfort I find from him, I lay awake well into the night. My insides are completely twisted; it's difficult to navigate the very real possibility that Demon could be ripped from me once again, despite the short time I have had him back.

I will never regret what I did to get to the space we are today. Ultimately, the choice was taken from me when they shoved me into another body. They are the ones who should live with that regret. I do. however. feel something akin to grief for the witches whose bodies I've taken and ruined. After all, they were just as innocent as we were.

This body, Reem Mori, was the only one who was cognizant and aware of what I was and what needed to be done. It was an uneasy relationship we'd formed, and for a while I assumed we could co-exist in one body. But Reem pulled back and eventually opted to die. I never understood why the sudden change of heart; we had worked together for years. But now I wonder if she knew her sister held the magic and, in the end, couldn't stomach what we would need to do.

Not many people can stomach the things that must be done. People like to say they will do whatever it takes, give grand speeches and shows of strength, but when it comes down to it no one wants to get their hands dirty. No one will choose to suffer for the greater good.

Sleep continues to evade me, the clock in my head getting louder and louder. Pushing up and away from Demon, I extract myself from the bed, pulling on leggings and a sports bra before heading down the stairs into the kitchen. The scent of coffee is already floating in the air.

Rounding the corner, I find Dios and Ava's brother are awkwardly glaring at each other from either side of the counter. Dios has a beer in his hand already, the other man holds a steaming cup of coffee.

Glaring at both, I grab my coffee before plopping myself onto the cool tiled floor with the cup in hand.

"Don't mind me," I grumble. "Continue onward with this odd standoff you two have." I gesture between the two. Dios cuts me a look but stays silent. The blond, however, lets out a long breath before he starts tapping his leg in a rhythmic pattern. "Do you have to do that?" I ask.

His cheeks redden and he looks down at his coffee, as if hoping he could crawl into the cup. "Sorry. Bad habit." He looks sheepish as he scratches the back of his neck. "I'm Jackson, by the way."

Demon rounds the corner, distracting me from the king of Hell, his auburn hair messy from bed and his chest bare. My eyes devour him. Bending down, he plants a kiss on top of my head before grabbing his cup of caffeine. "Well, this is a jolly kitchen," he mutters. I snort a laugh.

"Yes, well, for once it's not me. The tension was here when I wandered in," I respond.

His blue eyes cast between his friend and the king, who looks exhausted. "You are..." my mate asks the newcomer.

"Jackson, but I prefer Jax. Sorry to drop in like I did..."

I snort. "You saved the bar from watching Demon fuck me within an inch of my life."

Demon grabs my hair hard. "Behave."

Jackson clears his throat awkwardly. His cheeks are now even more red.

"Aww, you're kind of adorable, little King," I say from behind the steam of my coffee.

"Why are you here?" Demon asks Jax as he glares at me. The look has me squeezing my thighs together.

Jax sets his cup down, shoving his hands into his pockets. "My magic drew me here. I hadn't intended to open a portal here but," he casts a look towards Dios who says nothing, "my powers decided this was the safest place to dump me."

"And why would your magic bring you here? You've never met us," I reply. My eyes flick between the two men. "Or is there a secret romance here?"

Dios says nothing, his eyes locked on the king.

"It's. . ." The hesitation in him flares, looking to Dios for guidance.

"It doesn't matter to the situation at hand," Dios speaks for him. The king seems to sag with relief. The tension melts from him, even if for a brief moment.

I drain the last little bit of my coffee in my mug, ignoring the burn as it goes down. "Well," I start. "I'm Kallen, and this is my mate Demon. You obviously know Dios."

Jax's silver eyes are pools of flame against his skin as he inclines his head in a nod towards us by way of greeting.

Pushing up from the floor, I dust off my backside. "What can you tell us about The Order?"

The room suddenly vibrates with power, the air rippling around us. My gaze locks on the king, his silver eyes whirling to black and back to silver until Dios puts a strong hand on the back of his neck.

"*Mi ceilo*, breath." The small amount of pressure Dios applies has Jackson's eyes fluttering closed while his power finally recedes. "Good boy," Dios murmurs before releasing his neck.

I fan myself with my hand. "Damn, Dios. You have me wanting to be a good girl."

Demon growls, his hand grabbing a fist full of my hair. "You aren't a good girl Kallen, don't start now. Brat."

I preen under his attention. "Mmm. But I could be good… so, so good. With the right motivation."

Behind us, Dios mutters in Spanish before Jax clears his throat. "The Order killed the previous king of Hell, my father. I've been hunting them down but it's been. . . difficult, to say the least."

I cross my arms, leaning against Demon. "Why is it so difficult?"

He lets out a long sigh as his hands push through his hair. "They are good at disappearing and being elusive. Always have been, but it's seemingly gotten worse through the years. Every-time I get close, they are gone again. I have no way of getting to their leaders."

"Well, we need some type of plan. The vision I had involved

The Order invading, and I'm not looking to have that shit come true."

Jax furrows his brow. "Tell me everything. *Now.*"

Demon

Stepping through the portal she created, Dios, Jackson, Kallen, and I move back into the clubhouse in the late afternoon. After spending the morning getting on the same page regarding our intel, I want nothing more than to bury my cock in Kallen and fall asleep with my knot in her. And yet, I'm being assaulted by the smell of beer and wolf instead.

"Pres," Rucker says, walking up towards us and effectively ruining my day dream. The side eye he sends towards Kallen isn't missed either. I can already feel the tension headache forming. "We are ready for Church."

He starts to walk past me towards those doors that have become a barrier between Kallen and I. Anger and annoyance already start to pepper our bond as she looks at those fucking doors. "Kallen and Jackson will be joining us." The statement is out of my mouth before I can second guess it.

Anger washes through the air. "They aren't part of the club, they have no right to be in there" Rucker growls, his wolf dangerously close to the surface. It's not the first time lately I've wondered if I made the wrong choice appointing him to be VP, given how often he questions me.

"Kallen is my mate, so as far as I'm concerned, she is above club *and* pack law. Jackson is. . ." Glancing over at the king, I wonder just how much he wants me to share. When he gives a subtle nod, I keep talking. "Jackson is the king of Hell. Both will be present during this conversation because they have more information on what's happening than we do." I step forward, crowding his space. "I'm getting tired of you questioning everything I say. You aren't the president of this club, or the alpha of this pack. *I am.*"

"Maybe that needs to change," he snarls. "Maybe leadership isn't suited for you anymore, now that you have that golden pussy. Care to share? Maybe if I stick my cock in her, I'll under—." I don't let him finish before my fist connects with his jaw, a deep crimson hazing over my vision. His head snaps back and blood sprays from his split lip.

"Don't you *ever* talk about my mate that way," I bellow, drawing the attention of everyone. Pack members file into the room as my VP and I circle each other. "You want to challenge me for my position here? Fine. But you utter one thing about Kallen and I will rip your fucking throat out. Then, for shits and giggles, I'll fuck her on top of your dying body."

Behind me, I can hear Kallen let out a sigh of longing. "Promises, promises," she murmurs.

Rucker spits blood to the floor before wiping his mouth with the back of his hand. "We all had to earn this vest, but she just walks in here and suddenly we have to respect her?!" Lunging forward, he shifts rapidly into his wolf before tackling me to the ground, his claw digging into my shoulders while his teeth snap inches from my throat.

"Oh, for fucks sake," Kallen yells. From the corners, darkness bleeds out as her Hellbeasts move in. "Break them up will you boys?" Rucker's wolf backs off immediately as the creatures move forward, placing their massive black bodies between us. Green saliva pools from their mouths as they roll their lips back into a snarl. Kallen prances forward with all the confidence in the world as she stands before Rucker's wolf.

"Okay, my little bratty VP. What is it you need to see from me to convince you I'm on your side?"

Rucker shifts back to human form, his mouth still swollen and bleeding. "Fuck you, *whore*," he spats.

"Try again," she growls. "And think long and hard before

you say anything. Many men have gone toe-to-toe with me and none have survived, save one. And he's only alive because of his mate. That little piece of leather on your body won't protect you from me."

"That! That right there is why I won't trust you. You are threatening me." His voice takes on a high-pitched whine and I can only shake my head.

Kallen pinches the bridge of her nose. "Seriously, a toddler has more balls than you do." She leans around his frame towards the rest of the pack, which has now gathered in its entirety. "Okay friends, it's clear this one is a twat, but I'm going to assume the rest of you just want to know I'm genuine about being here?" Some nods move through the crowd. "Wonderful. Then I have the perfect idea!"

Kallen turns away from the crowd before leaning down and planting a kiss on me. "At least this helps with a future solstice gift! I'll send one of my beasts to you when I'm ready." Before I can grab her, she's through a shimmering portal.

My heart plummets into my stomach as her disappearance triggers fear and anxiety that I'll never see her again. Pushing up, I rush over to Rucker, slamming my fist into his face hard. "If anything happens to her, I'll skin you alive," I growl. I move to punch him again, but Dios intercepts me.

"It's done," he mutters. He holds my stare, waiting to see if I'm going to push back against him as well. Once satisfied that I'm not going to attempt to murder him, Dios turns his back to me and directs the club to take Rucker to the holding cells downstairs. No one dares to argue.

A bottle of beer appears in front of me. Jackson offers me a smile as he drinks his own.

"You wanna tell me how you two know each other?" I ask as Dios moves back over to us.

They look at each other, locked in some silent battle before

Jax lets out a sigh. "It sounds dumb. I know it does. But from our dreams." His cheeks flush slightly as he says it.

I arch my eyebrow at Dios. "Seriously?"

He shrugs. "That's as simple of a story you'll get. So yes. From our dreams."

He pushes past me and Jackson, settling against the bar as he's handed a shot and bottle of beer to match my own. "So now what?" he asks, looking between me and his dream man.

Shoving my hand through my hair, ignoring the burn from my busted knuckles, I shake my head. "Fuck if I know. I can feel her still, down our bond, so I suppose we wait."

"Aren't you worried?" Jackson asks. "We should go after her, right?"

Dios snorts and I cut him a hard look before I shake my head. "You can't control a force of nature like that. She'll get us when she's ready."

SEVEN

Kallen

(Ava Maria- Tommee Proffitt and Stanaj)

Every few feet, a golden sconce is fixed to the wall holding a glass vase and flickering candles. The soft light casts a warm glow into the long hallway. The house had smelled like evergreen and cinnamon upon my entry; now the air is awash with the metallic scent of blood.

My whistle echoes down the long dark hallway as I meander towards my query. My bare feet are silent on the marble floor, my high heels discarded outside before entering the home. Blood is so hard to get off suede, but delightfully easier to get off skin. And given the footprints I'm leaving behind me, I made the right choice to remove them. My white dress, however, is beautifully destroyed with festive blood splatter across it. *Demon is going to love this so much.*

"There is something that is just so festive about getting revenge for your mate. Puts one in the mood. If you know what I mean," I say to the wolf shifter who is currently dragging his body away from me.

"You're fucking crazy!" he cries. His left leg is bent at an unnatural angle and blood seeps from multiple wounds on his body.

Rolling my eyes, I leap in front of him. "How unoriginal." Yanking him upwards by his dirty hair, I squat down so we are face to face. "I'm not *crazy*, I'm just...feral? Yes. I think I like that better." I grin wide at the true fear the man before me emits. His screams ring through the halls as I start the process of killing him. I make it slow, painful, and exquisite. I saved him for last so he could watch me work the rest of the pack over. *Luke.* The pack alpha. The one who caused my mate the most problems. A low gurgle and groan come from his throat as he chokes on his blood, cutting off the screams.

Standing up, I look down at my handiwork as I hum along to the jolly beat of music playing from the living room. A shadow moves up next to me, and my Hellbeast drops his head down to nuzzle me. "Go get Demon, will you, my lovely?"

Rounding the corner, I drag the last, carved up member of the Feral Riders MC into the giant living room with the rest of the bodies, discarding the dead shifter next to the doorway. Looking around with my hands on my ample hips, I bring my arm up and wipe the blood off my mouth. The fire in the corner crackles, illuminating the couch and two armchairs. Overall it's a comfortable space; the bodies add a sprinkle of macabre to the atmosphere..

I let out a long breath as I look down at the pile of worthless males. "You know how to get a girl to break a sweat." I pause and laugh to myself. "I'm probably the only girl you've ever caused to sweat," I mutter to the room of bodies.

Leaning down to the small bag I brought in, I grab the red and green bow and stick it atop/ my head in the center of my braid. I move to sit on the couch, making sure the top lace of my dress is expertly open just enough to show off my cleavage. When I'm sure it's all perfect, I allow my magic to unfold. The shimmering portal I open exposes my beautiful mate along with Jax and Dios, all three stepping through.

For a moment, Demon's eyes are wild as they rapidly search for me. When he sees me, his body relaxes only slightly. "Jesus, Kallen," he huffs. His blue eyes track around the room, digesting the sight of the blood and bodies.

I shrug. "What? I missed so many holidays with you, I figured this was a good gift to make up for the solstices we didn't get to celebrate!" I fling my arms wide, indicating the carnage around me before gesturing down my body. "It's also killing two birds with one stone; the pack can't possibly think I have nefarious intentions when I've now killed all your rivals."

"Your mate is a little bloodthirsty, Demon," Dios snorts, and I smile wide at his assessment.

"At least we don't have to worry about these fucks anymore," Demon replies, crossing his arms over his chest. "And Rucker can shut the fuck up." I devour the view of him; his leather cut slung over a thermal long sleeve, auburn hair pulled back low in a bun exposing his freckled face and brilliant blue eyes. "You done eye fucking me?"

"I'll never be done eye fucking you." Glancing at Jackson, I wince. "Gods, you and your sister look alike."

"I've heard that my whole life." His voice is rich and layered with authority. He looks more at ease than when I left. His messy blonde hair frames those telltale eyes, but unlike his sister, his frame is massive. Muscular arms peak out from a buffalo print flannel and shapely legs are covered in jeans. I think I see tattoos peeking out from his chest. His gaze tracks around the room as he takes in the bloodshed. They don't heat like Demon's do, but they also don't shy away from it.

Demon moves into the room, sitting down next to me before pulling me onto his lap. "I missed you," he says as he nuzzles into my neck. "Don't you ever disappear like that again." When he nips at our mating mark, I let out a moan and feel my body light up like a fucking Christmas tree. My scent no doubt fills the room based on the rumble from my mate.

Dios sits down adjacent to me in one of the armchairs and sheds his leather cut, his widespread legs sporting black jeans with a tight white t-shirt that exposes his rich brown skin. Tattoos swirl all over his body, including over his shaved head. Jax follows closely behind, heading towards the other unoccupied chair. Dios watches him cross in front of us, his mismatched aqua and forest eyes filled with lust.

My mind is flooded with the idea of those two together, followed by the idea of us joining. Demon huffs out a chuckle as if he knows exactly where my mind went. His hand slowly snakes between my legs and rips them apart. I let out a small gasp, the other two men looking over at us.

"It would seem my mate here sees something she likes," Demon quips gruffly, his voice a lover's caress down my spine. He strokes over my core; the thin undergarments are doing nothing to hide how wet I've gotten. *Let's be honest, I chose this outfit in hopes Demon would fuck me here.*

Dios cocks an eyebrow at me before licking his lips and looking up at Jackson. "What do you say, do you want to play with them?"

Jax looks at the Latino man, fire reflected in those silver eyes before he shocks me and drops to his knees in front of Dios. "Please," his voice shakes in a hushed tone. The strain of his cock is evident through his pants.

"*Buen chico*. Good boy."

Something about a man speaking another language makes my pussy gush every time. I let out a low moan as Demon shoves my panties aside in a swift motion, allowing him access to my wet core.

"She's soaked already," Demon hums as he plays with my slick folds.

"Rules?" Dios asks the two of us. My eyes roll back in my head as Demon expertly strokes my clit. His lips trace up and down my neck, briefly catching on my mate mark again. It makes my hips buck, his fingers plunging deep into me before he pulls back out and continues his lazy assault.

"Do we have rules, *mo chreach bheag?*" His breath is hot against my ear.

I laugh wickedly. "I don't know if we've ever had rules, my *Deamhan*. Why start now?" I grind my ass down onto his hard cock under me. He lets out a grunt and I grin.

"So no limits?' he hedges.

I pause for a moment. "Demon is the only one who can call me names. No one else is allowed to call me a whore or slut unless you wanna die."

Dios mutters something under his breath that sounds oddly like he is praising a god. He looks at Jackson who is still kneeling and growls, "Take her clothing off. I want to see everything."

Demon

I gently shove Kallen up off my lap as Jackson walks

towards her. I don't move. I know the drill. I relent to Dios when we play; he knows my limits and doesn't push them. Kallen's arousal is filling the small space, making my cock painfully hard in my pants. Grabbing onto it, I shift to relieve pressure as Jackson's fingers start to unlace the corset holding Kallen into her dress. In no time at all, he has my mate stripped down and standing in all her curvy glory in the low fire light.

"Well, you've got me undressed, Dios. What now?" She pops her hand onto her hip, ever the brat. Dios only smirks at her, not one to be rushed or give in to a brat.

"*Mi cielo*, touch her cunt. Tell me how wet she is," Dios commands. His eyes flash as his wolf prowls to the surface. Jackson hesitates for a moment, glancing towards me before I give a subtle nod of permission to touch my mate.

"It's my cunt you are going to be touching, why are you looking at him for permission?" Kallen snaps.

"She has a fair point," I say, though my wolf feels far more territorial.

Dios lets out a low growl. "I believe our dear king was making sure the other predator in the room had some control. We know how mates are."

Kallen rolls her eyes as she positions herself off to the side on the couch. I'm perched on it so both Dios and I have a view. We watch Jackson drop down in front of her, slipping his middle finger into her.

"Fuckkk, she's soaking." He bites his lip and groans, before continuing to pump in and out of her lazily. Slowly, his other hand creeps up and grasps her left breast, eliciting a moan from deep in my mate's throat. She keeps those evergreen eyes locked on me even as a flush crawls up her pale skin and her breathing gets heavy. Jackson brings his lips to her neck, sucking and kissing up and down it. His movements are feverish and hungry as if he's lost himself in her.

Dios is up in a flash, pulling back on Jackson's dirty blond hair. "Did I tell you to fuck her with your fingers?" He growls.

Jackson lets out a whimpered, "No, Sir." I groan as I watch Dios grab the finger that was just inside Kallen and lick it clean.

"Fuck, she tastes good. Like sin and salvation." He releases Jackson and sits back down, beckoning Jax to follow him. He obediently listens and curls between his spread legs, head resting on his thigh as he gently strokes the outline of Dios's hard cock. The two clearly have some type of bond.

It's always the ones who have the most responsibility who need the act of submission, isn't it?

"Is someone going to make me cum?" Kallen demands. "We have all this dick in here but yet I'm still empty. Or should I just do this myself?" She smirks as she trails her hand down and begins playing with clit. I growl low, a warning for her to play nice, to behave. She lets out a feral noise back at me, snapping her teeth in my direction.

"Demon, your mate has fire in her. I want to watch you stuff that pretty cunt until she can't speak and when you're done, you fill her to the brim. I want my pretty little puppet to lick it out of her until she covers his face with her release." Jackson lets out a whimper of need and Kallen's eyes light up with a savage delight.

"What about you?" Jax asks, peering up at Dios like he truly is a god. *If he only knew.*

Dios grins wickedly. "I'm going to be fucking you in the ass while you eat her pussy. And *only* once the rest of us have come will you be allowed to finish. Understand?" Jackson nods eagerly. "Good. Now take my cock out and suck it while we watch Demon fuck the brat out of his mate."

I get to work removing my shirt as Kallen saunters over to me, her hands trailing up and down her body. My cock springs free of the confines of my pants and she kneels before me, sucking the tip between her lips and playing with the piercing as she does. The sound that rips from my throat is animalistic as she works my shaft in her mouth, her fingers cupping my balls. I grip her hair hard, pulling it free from the braid she's had it in and force her to keep pace with me. My focus remains on her as I relentlessly fuck her warm mouth. She moans out, the vibration moving up and down my shaft.

Fucking hell, I'm not going to last. I pull myself free of her mouth and spin her around so she can face Dios and Jackson. Lining her up, I feed her pussy my cock slowly.

"Oh, fuckkk," she moans as I slide into her. I allow my eyes to trail over to my sergeant-at-arms and Jackson, feral need displayed across both expressions.

"Look at how hungry you are making them," I groan as I thrust into her. "They like watching my cock disappear into your tight cunt. They want to watch as I fill you up, as I breed you." She lets out a long moan, her head thrown back as I lift her hips up and down, fucking my cock deep into her.

"How does she feel?" Dios asks, his voice tight as though he is trying to contain himself.

I smile, my fingers playing with her clit. "Like she was fucking meant to be stuffed full of my cock." I feel her pussy quiver around me, the walls tightening. "Do you like that? Like hearing how your pussy feels?"

"Yes. Yes, I like how you talk. I like knowing what I do to you," she pants. Barely hanging onto her sanity, her head is thrown back and her eyes are closed.

Grabbing her chin, I force her to look over at Dios and Jackson. "Look what you do to them, *mo chreach bheag.*" Both men look enthralled by my mate bouncing on my cock.

"Oh fuck, that's so hot. Fuck, I need to cum. Fill me up. I want it dripping out of me while Jackson eats my pussy," she cries out, picking up the pace herself and fucking me hard.

I place my mouth over the mating mark, licking it before

commanding, "I need to feel you cum. Squeeze my dick while I fill you up." I bite down hard, one hand moving down and pressing into her clit. Her pussy spasms around me as she soaks my dick. My own release not far behind, my cock sends spurt after spurt of my release into her. Somewhere I can hear Dios muttering in Spanish, "*Mierda, mierda.* Fuck, fuck."

The feeling of her around me is divine. Our mate-bond is pulsing. I'm too far gone to notice my knot has swelled and is pushing inside her, locking us together. "Fuck Kallen, sorry *mo chreach bheag,* I didn't plan on knotting you here." The feeling of her around me has my eyes rolling back in my head.

"Oh my god, I feel so fucking full," Kallen moans as she palms her breasts. "Fuck, fuck, fuck Demon. You feel so damn good."

"Careful calling out to a god, you never know who is listening," Dios mumbles.

I cut him a sharp look before I feel Kallen relax onto me.

Dios smirks at me before looking down at Jackson. "*Mi cielo,* go clean her up," he commands.

"Yes, Sir." Jackson starts to crawl towards us. I'm well aware he'll now be cleaning her up around my knot. Dios leans forward, his mismatched eyes blazing with hunger. He pulls his shirt over his head, revealing his muscular body and whirling tattoos in a language long dead. Yanking his cock from his boxers, he swiftly kicks away his pants, leaving him fully naked in the glow of the fire.

I'm pulled from looking at him at the first feel of Jackson's tongue where I'm still joined with Kallen. She bucks forward, gripping his hair hard as he laps up the mess we've made before moving to her clit. My cock pulses inside her as her cunt squeezes me.

"Fucking hell. I'm going to cum again," I groan and another wave of cum paints the inside of her. Jackson moans his approval as Kallen cries out.

"Mmmm. I assume you are well and truly locked into her?" Dios asks, stroking his thick cock. For a moment I feel bad for Jackson given how large Dios is. *And if he knots Jackson that will be even worse.* I nod in confirmation to his question, knowing at this point it's going to be a while before I release her. I watch as Dios pulls Jackson's head away from us, earning a whimper from Kallen. "Do you want me to fuck you now?"

"Yes, please. Give it to me. I need you so badly it hurts," Jackson practically cries. His mouth glistens from feasting on us. This man is a far cry from what I know of him.

"*Si, mi cielo.* You can have me. You beg so pretty for my cock, how could I refuse you?" The words are tender, and for a moment I wonder if Kallen and I should leave, but then she rocks her hips and I'm lost to that feeling again. Lost to the idea of filling her up over and over again. The primal part of me loves the idea of her being stuffed full of my release.

I watch Dios stroke his cock with a bottle of lube he produced from god knows where. When he feels adequately slick, he lines his dark head up against Jackson. Slowly, with more care than he's given any other lover, he pushes deep into Jax, who lets out a small cry at the intrusion.

"That's it, *mi cielo.* You take me so fucking good. Fuckkk." Dios stares transfixed where his cock is disappearing into Jackson before he pulls it back out again, allowing Jax to adjust to his girth.

"That is so fucking hot," Kallen pants as she eyes the two men before leaning back so her back is flush against my chest. "But not as hot as knowing it's your cock inside me. It's your knot holding us together. And it's your cum that's going to be dripping out of me for the rest of the day."

"Fuck I love you, *mo chreach bheag.*"

Neither of us are in a hurry to stop, but eventually my knot finally slips free and Kallen wraps her naked body around my own. When Dios finally allows Jackson to cum I almost feel bad for him, given how long he was edged. Paying no mind to the carnage we've just fucked in, Dios cradles Jax against his naked body.

After a few moments of silence, the four of us basking in the aftermath, Jackson finally speaks up. "Did I hear you slaughtered this whole MC for a solstice gift?"

Kallen lets out a giggle into my chest. "It was a bonus to gaining the club's trust." She pulls back, facing Jackson slightly. "And I think, given that you are here, we both know we need all the help we can get with what's to come."

Jackson's face is grim, reality slowly setting in. My eyes catch my sergeant-at-arms and we both know this will be one of our last peaceful moments before we suit up for battle.

I press a kiss to Kallen's temple. "Happy Solstice, *mo chreach bheag.*"

"Happy Solstice, my *Deamhan.*"

EIGHT

Katherine really made a fucking mess, but she did give me an inspired idea. The war has been going too slow for my liking, Alexi taking his sweet time hunting witches. But Katherine had an idea; a way for witches to volunteer to feed the vampires in a safe space. It'll be perfect. A way to hunt for my powers, kill the covens, and finally get my vengeance.

-Personal Journal of Kallen

Kallen

Dropping the head of the Feral Riders' president onto the ground of our clubhouse, the room goes silent. I kick it over to Rucker, who is balls-deep in club pussy. The girl riding him, to her credit, doesn't react and just slips off his dick, walking back over to the bar with a sashay of her hips. Gotta love a confident woman.

"Happy?" I ask as he pushes his still-hard cock back into his pants.

He doesn't say anything, but the look on his face gives me everything I need. *Checkmate.* I smirk at him, raising my eyebrow, daring him to challenge me.

Jackson and Dios move up behind me as Demon walks to the center of the room. "Does anyone else have an issue with my mate?" he roars. The room is damn near silent. No one is brave enough to utter a word. I smirk as I feel my phone buzz. Pulling it from my pocket, I look down at the illuminated screen.

Ciaran: We need to talk.

I roll my eyes before typing out a response.

Me: about what?

How he managed to get my phone number is beyond me, but thus far the little Vampire Viking hasn't said much other than telling me he has my number.

Ciaran: Astrea.

My blood is chilled for a moment. After everything I had done to them, there is only one reason Ciaran would seek my help.

Me: Where are you?

I watch as the text bubbles pop up then disappear rapidly. I almost think he is going to ignore me, that he is regretting texting me.

Ciaran: Meet at The Playground?

"Well boys, looks like we've got someone to meet." I glance at Jackson and narrow my eyes. "Except you – you need to stay."

"I'm not leaving him behind," Dios argues.

Planting my hands on my hips, I roll my eyes. "Look. We need to go meet someone, and that someone is most likely going to be with his sister," I say, jerking my head towards Jax. "So unless he wants a reunion, he's going to stay put."

Dios looks as though he is going to argue again, but Jackson cuts him off. "She's right. I can't see Ava yet. I'll be fine." Dios looks less than assured but relents with a nod.

"Wonderful!" I clap. "Let's have some fun!"

The music from the club pulses in time with my heartbeat. My skin feels electric as I walk into The Playground. Dios and Demon walk a step behind me, and I can feel the eyes of people on us as they stop on the MC cut both men are wearing. Primal Knights aren't typically seen in the city, much less the President and his sergeant at arms. The Feral Riders made sure of it.

Between Alexi and Shadow's father, the Feral Riders got the upper hand rapidly on all other MC's in the cities. The war was bloody and brutal for all, and in the end, it was the Primal Knights who retreated.

Alexi and Julian deserved to die much longer, bloodier deaths.

Demon grips my hand hard, dragging my awareness back to him and the space around us. Ava's club is beautiful. The reds and blacks of the room swirl together, giving it a warm and inviting feeling. The place feels free, as if every desire you have could come true. It's the exact opposite of what someone like her would be able to own in Hell. And in the center of the room is the princess herself in the lap of one of her dragons. Her head is thrown back, legs wide as he pumps his fingers in and out of her.

I let out a dark laugh. "Who knew the princess was such an exhibitionist?"

"That's Ava?" Demon asks.

I offer a smirk as I cross my arms. "That's her."

"You didn't say her mate was Drago," he growls low.

I side-eye him for a moment. "Does that matter?"

He drags his hand down his face, something akin to exhaustion creeping into his eyes. "The club and Drago haven't always been on good terms."

I raise my eyebrow at him. "So, I shouldn't add that Shadow is her other mate?"

"Fucking Christ," he grumbles, "that's worse."

Dios shakes his head, glaring at me and muttering something like, "You should have warned us."

I glare right back at him. "Do I want to know why?"

He shakes his head, thick tension now occupying his body.

The golden mating ring in his eye burns bright against the dim lights. "I'll tell you later."

I shrug, pulling Demon over to Dios, who has found a spot at the massive bar. Dios grabs a beer, handing the cool bottle to me. "She looks just like Jax," he says. I offer a small "Mhm" in response.

Signaling to the bartender for a shot, the tall man who had been previously helping Dios offers a nod and gestures to a newcomer to grab me the drink. The female has lilac hair cut short with a pair of headphones around her neck. Thick-rimmed black glasses perch on a pert freckled nose, and her curvy body is dressed in an off-the-shoulder band t-shirt and ripped jeans. When her body angles towards me, her eyes widen as her hand releases the shot to me.

Offering her a cocky smile, I shoot it back without a thought before looking at Dios. "I hope I don't need to remind you to keep your mouth shut to her that her brother is here." He doesn't respond, his eyes locked just beyond me.

"Dahlia?" The name leaves his mouth in a whisper.

Demon

Nothing could have prepared me for seeing Rucker's baby sister, covered in tattoos, serving drinks in Ava's bar. Her tiny nose flares, fear pushing through her scent as she nudges her round glasses up on her face. Dios and I stand frozen as Dahlia's eyes bounce between us and Kallen, before her body tenses as if she is about to flee.

"You boys are scaring her," Kallen growls. "Stop it."

Normally if Kallen gave a command, I would listen in a heartbeat, but I'm transfixed by the ghost of my past. A thousand questions bubble up, begging to be released.

A female comes up from behind, snaking their arm around

Dahlia's curvy waist. Her body visibly relaxes as the person presses a kiss to her temple. "Are they bothering you?" they ask while glaring at us.

Dahlia doesn't say anything, only offering a soft smile before shaking her head no. The newcomer narrows their eyes as if they don't believe it before stepping out from behind her, effectively shielding Dahlia from us.

"Dahlia, is it?" Kallen steps between us. Her body provides a barrier between us and them.

"Who wants to know?" The woman's dark skin shimmers with hints of gold decorating her cheekbones and eyelids. Shiny dark lip gloss is painted on full lips and her hair falls long in thick dark braids.

Kallen smiles. "My name is Kallen. I assume these two hulking piles of muscles behind me are already known to your girlfriend behind you." Kallen leans over the bar closer, her eyes trailing up and down the person. "Now, who are you?"

"Bast," she says, her eyes seeming to shift between golden orbs and luminous white. Dahlia peeks over her shoulder.

"Well, lovely to meet you, Bast. This is Dios and Demon, in case *you* don't know them."

She sneers at us. "I know who they are, and you all should know I won't allow you to touch a hair on her head. Now enjoy your drinks and leave before I tell Drago you are here."

I go to open my mouth, to command this lost wolf to stay so she can explain herself, but Kallen squeezes my hand hard. "Will do, lovely, we are just here to meet a friend. We'll be on our way once we are done," she says, turning me around so I'm facing the stage again.

Her nails dig into my palm, sending jolts of sharp pain through me. "I don't know who that is to you both, but you're going to get it together right now or I'm doing this on my own," she snarls in a hushed tone.

My reaction is slow at best as I drag my eyes to hers. Words dry up in my mouth, and I only give her a quick nod. My gaze skates to Dios for a moment, and I can see his mouth is set in a grim line.

In one fell swoop, our past has come back to haunt us.

Kallen

The two men are vibrating with emotion as we watch Ava get off on her mate's lap, before they lock eyes with the vampire we've come to meet. "We can't go up there while Drago is here," Demon says.

I don't have to look to know that Demon is wrestling for control with his wolf right now. There is a history that I'm missing here. A lot of fucking history. "That's fine, we'll wait. Ciaran won't leave without talking to us. And when we are through here, you two are going to give me the low down on what the fuck is going on – as well as tell me who that girl was."

"It's not a good idea to stay here long," Dios grunts. "Even with the Feral Riders gone, this is still *his* territory." He jerks his head towards Drago.

Frowning, I take a sip of the beer in front of me. Seeing the hesitation in both Dios and Demon reminds me how long it's been since I've had anyone at my side. Caution isn't something I use, not since everything happened with the original families. Something in my brain broke that day, and over the years it's rewired into what I am today.

My evergreen eyes track the crowd around me before landing back on my mate. He's stiff, ready to spring into action. My own body feels loose, almost bored. The startling difference between us, between me and anyone really, seems to be that I thrive in chaos and confrontation.

"Drago won't do shit," I finally mutter back to Dios. "And if he does, I've been wanting to play anyway."

"He isn't the dragon I'm worried about." Dios responds.

Shadow. "Ah. You are worried about nothing, then. That one is too preoccupied with his demons to show up here."

The dragon that Alexi tormented for so long. Most people think Alexi broke him and remade him. But Alexi just provided the mold; Shadow was broken long before Alexi got his fangs into him. Shadow has had a death wish from the moment I saw him dragged into that aviary.

From the dark, I watch as the guards drag the unconscious young dragon into the giant cage. It seems like overkill. At least, until the wind shifts and I catch the scent of his magic. Now the glittering collar on his neck and cage around him makes sense.

One of my beasts moves up behind me, nudging my hand. I pat it lightly on the head before slinking out towards the unconscious mass. His dark hair is moved over his face, but it does nothing to hide the years of scars on him. Some look to be self-inflicted, while others are the handiwork of someone else.

"Do you like my new pet?" Alexi's cloying voice moves in behind me.

Another shift in the wind brings a secondary scent to me, and my eyes flair. "What's your plan here, Alexi?" My voice is quiet in the large space. "You took a mated dragon. This won't end well." It takes everything in me not to drive a knife through his heart right now. The idea of feeling his blood slip through my fingers as I drain him sends goosebumps over my body. His days are numbered.

He snorts. "He's not mated. The Rosewood alpha sold him to me. We can test out the collars on him; it's all he's good for."

Turning my head, I lock onto Alexi, the dark hair I have right now shifting over my shoulder. "I had hoped you would be smarter, given the long life you've lived. But it appears having a cock sucks the intelligence out no matter what." His face turns red with anger, and I roll my eyes as I walk towards him. *"Mark my words, Alexi, his mate will come for him. And when he is free, you won't survive."*

From that moment on, Alexi made it his mission to break Shadow apart. And the young dragon allowed him to do just that.

Demon's hand on my lower back pulls me from my thoughts. "He's leaving," he murmurs into my ear.

Without a word, the three of us move up the stairs toward where Ciaran sits. Walking in, we realize he isn't alone. Ava is perched on a chair next to him. When her eyes lock on us, they flare only for a moment.

"Hello, little *princesa*," Dios purrs, his accent thick against his tongue. She stiffens slightly, her body coiling inward. *"Estas muy lejos de casa."*

I turn around, smacking him in the chest. "Dios, leave her. We are here for Ciaran." I look back to Ava, my eyes locking with hers. A strange understanding passes between us; two people who have seen a devastating future and are keeping it from those around us. "Ava has enough she'll need to face without your bullshit."

Ciaran pushes to a stand as he looks to Ava. "Thank you for the drink. Tell Drago I'll call him." He looks back at us. "Let's go get this over with. I'm not looking forward to how angry Astrea will be about this."

Oh, this just got interesting. I open a portal and Ciaran walks directly through it before Demon follows. Dios remains next to me as I look at the princess.

My eyes narrow on her. "We need your magic if we are going to win this," I warn.

"I know," she says simply.

Crossing my arms over my chest, I take in her scent. Her magic is still low. "So what are you doing about it?"

A growl slips from her. "Everything I can," she spits out.

I only nod my head. The battle she is up against in getting Shadow to let go of his past is almost as big as the one we are fighting.

Stepping through the portal, I drop us into a clearing far from Astrea. I turn to Dios and quietly say "I need you to go back."

"For what?" he asks, clearly confused.

"I think you need to talk to Jax about what his intentions are. Ava is already struggling, and if you add a surprise visit from her brother, I'm not sure how helpful that'll be"

He lets out a long sigh, dragging his hand down his face before nodding.

"Great!" I open two portals, one to the clubhouse and one towards Astrea. When Dios walks through his, I close it before following Ciaran and Demon through ours. There's no turning back…

NINE

Demon

The moment Kallen's feet hit the grass outside the isolated cabin, the world explodes into black glittering mist. My mate's laughter rings unhinged through the air even as my eyes attempt to seek her out. My wolf bristles under my skin, barely contained as he tries to push out and protect our mate.

"Oh, Astrea, you are getting good with that magic." I can hear her move to the left of me, but the magic is so thick even my hand in front of my face is invisible. "But I don't think you are as good as I was."

"You fucking bitch." Another voice hisses from the dark. "I'm going to kill you."

"*Kamerate.*" Ciaran's hard voice cuts through the darkness, a

97

faint glowing light suddenly appearing before it flares so bright that I'm forced to close my eyes. When it fades, I find the dark magic cleared. The vampire has his arms braced around a curvy female, her eyes the same evergreen as Kallen's. She thrashes a little against the hold of her mate.

I feel Kallen move up beside me, her arm linking with mine. "Ciaran, you've gotten good with that little light trick," she purrs. "But judging by the unhinged way your mate just went after me, I doubt you've figured out how to truly use it."

Astrea lunges, despite the fact that Ciaran is holding her so tightly her ribs would be cracked if she were mortal. "You have no business being here!" she screams.

"That's not what your mate thought when he texted me."

"Gods damn it, Kallen," I mutter as I watch Astrea go still in the vampire's arms.

"You did what?" she hisses.

Ciaran spins her so he's holding her via the throat, looking directly into her eyes. "We aren't getting anywhere. This magic is taking hold of you, and I won't lose you to it. Kallen is our best shot. So you are going to play nicely, both of you, and we are going to fucking figure this out." For a moment I think she's going to fight him more, but her hands unclench, and she gives a subtle nod. He waits a beat before releasing Astrea and allowing her to turn towards us.

Kallen lets out a dramatic sigh, as if this were boring her. "Ciaran, you should have just let us fight." Gesturing towards me, she continues. "Whatever, I guess we have time later. Anyway, Astrea and Ciaran, this is my mate Demon."

Ciaran eyeballs my vest. "You're with the Primal Knights."

"I *am* the Primal Knights," I respond with authority, my wolf peering out from my eyes.

Kallen purrs next to me. "Fuck, you make me wet when you do that."

"Gods," Astrea mutters in disgust.

"Astrea and I haven't mastered the magic yet; without her grimoire, we are running into issues. My mothers isn't complete," Ciaran explains.

Kallen snorts. "Kara was a lot of things, but the Carmines had no idea what they were doing when they created The Harbinger magic, much less the magic they infused with your natural ones."

Astrea frowns. "What do you mean? I thought the only magic he had was what Kara gave him."

"Tsk, tsk…Ciaran, you didn't tell your mate where that kernel of original magic came from?" Kallen quips in mock horror.

The way the air stills around us has me jerking Kallen hard into my body. Two snakes move off of Astrea's body, their shadow forms twisting and curling around her until they drop to the ground in full corporeal form. One is so dark, it gobbles up the light around us; the other is iridescent, its black scales popping out with some hints of rainbow when the light catches it.

My mouth brushes the shell of Kallen's ear. "Did you *have* to launch a grenade into this?"

Her body shakes with unbridled laughter. "Why, yes. Yes, I did."

<hr>

Kallen

"What is she talking about?" Astrea asks, turning back to her mate. Ciaran shoots me a glare over her head before pushing his hand down the side of his shaved head. "We promised no more secrets, Ciaran." Astrea's voice sounds sad.

"I knew of my magic before this, or at least some of it. It was bound by my mother when I was younger. She took the memory of it, locking the magic away. After she died, my memories came back. But the magic stayed locked away. I think she did it as a failsafe, however, to prevent me from following through with a request someone had of me."

"Which was what?"

"I remained in Gothic Grove after my mother died at the request of my half-brother. He is the leader of an organization."

I snort. "You mean a fucking cult," I snarl.

Another glare shot my way. "Fine. Yes. It's a cult now, but it didn't used to be," Ciaran replies in exasperation.

"Bullshit. The Order has always been an issue to Hell," I counter. "Their group was an issue even when I wasn't in this body. Their leaders are power-hungry old men."

Astrea looks between us, anger brewing on her face and her evergreen eyes are practically flaming. Magic pulses from her in uncontrolled waves; her whole body shaking in an attempt to keep it contained. It tells me everything I need to know about where she is at.

Taking three steading breaths, she finally goes to speak. "Okay, okay. You need to keep explaining, Ciaran, or I'm going to lose my shit. You have a half brother?"

"My father is from Hell, or rather, he was. He's dead now. My half brother was raised in Hell within The Order, whereas my mother never had any intention of allowing them to get their hooks into me. She would have failed if I hadn't befriended Shadow or found you. When I came of age, she saw my powers emerge and knew someone would come looking for me, so she bound them. It wasn't long before he did appear. His influence was rather insidious; he convinced me to help him take Gothic Grove."

Astrea narrows her eyes. "What was his end goal?"

Ciaran hesitates for a moment before continuing. "He was looking for someone, and I was to find her."

"Ava," Astrea breathes out. "He was looking for Ava."

Ciaran nods. "Yes. But by the time I found her, I had already met and rescued Shadow. I had no interest in abandoning the city. When he started the mate bond with her, I couldn't rip them from each other. My half-brother showed his true colors after that; he was furious when I began to pull away. Meeting you only made me dig deeper into that resolve. I knew I needed to keep you away from him."

"Why?"

"Because he needs power. And if he couldn't get Ava, you would be his next target. Like Hell would I let him touch you," Ciaran snarls.

Demon makes a noise, pulling the attention of the two. "He's *vacío*." Ciaran frowns, confused by the term Demon uses. "It means someone who has no magic, someone who has to feed off the magic of others to gain power," he explains. "Or at least, that's what a friend of mine would call him."

"How is that different from Ava?" I ask, leaving out her brother's name. "She gains magic from her mates."

Demon shrugs, replying, "I'm not the one to ask. I think you know who we need to talk to."

I roll my eyes. "Fine," I huff.

Astrea refocuses on Ciaran. "So, you realized your half-brother is a fucking power hunger twat and pulled away," she accuses.

He chuckles and nods. "Yes. But more so I realized this city was *mine* and my families. I wasn't going to turn it over to him."

"But wait…you were shocked by your mother's letter when we were on my family's grounds. That felt like a genuine reaction. There wasn't a lie," Astrea questions.

He grimaces slightly. "The letter unlocked my magic; the kernel of Hell magic alongside the witch magic she gave me to help you. So I was shocked, but mainly by the power I felt coursing through me."

Astrea, for her part, doesn't look nearly as angry as I would have been. Ciaran moves towards her, cupping her face with his hand. "I'm sorry. I should have told you. I fucked up," he pleads, and the sincerity is palpable.

For a long moment she doesn't say anything; her breathing is steady and the snakes remain curled up against her legs as if waiting to strike despite it being her mate. Finally, she turns those piercing emerald eyes to me, stepping away from Ciaran's hold.

"So how does the fact that he holds Hell magic impact this whole thing?" she asks me.

Pushing out of Demon's hold, I walk towards her, testing her boundaries. She is unyielding as she stands toe-to-toe with me and again, I'm furious with her family for ruining a friendship that could have been something wonderful. If only my soul had been in someone other than her sister; maybe we could get past this resentment she holds, but looking at your dead sister's body does not make one want to be friends.

"I'm not sure, honestly. The Harbinger magic, inherently, is dark. It was born from a place of revenge and grief." I pause for a moment; this is the part that Demon has never heard. "Look, can we get a drink or something? This next part of this whole story is rather bloody. Trust me, you're going to need it."

TEN

Kallen

The cabin the two are staying in is small but cozy.. The windows are thrown open, coaxing the evergreen-scented breeze inward. The air is scented with smoke and wood from the fire cracking in the hearth. Magic seems to infuse the air, keeping the chill out where the warmth of the flames can't reach. Ciaran hands Demon a crystal tumbler of dark amber liquid while Astrea walks over to me with a giant glass of wine that matches her own. I eagerly take it, gulping the sweet liquid down my throat.

"Okay, time for an origin story. And please don't have your snakes try to eat me for any of this. I didn't choose this, your family did. Plus, I don't want any of my wolves to have to try and go head-to-head with them. That would just get bloody and honestly time consuming," I offer with a touch of humor in my tone.

She only gives me a nod before curling herself onto Ciaran's lap.

"Even before The Harbinger magic, I was powerful. I was, and still am, the only witch to have Hellbeasts as my familiars – not just one, but a pack. That was unheard of in the witch community. My mother and her piece of shit husband took that as meaning I was some evil spawn. I fled my family home as soon as I could. Demon and I made a life together, away from their insidious goals." Demon growls low next to me, no doubt the memories of the night he found me playing across his mind. "Demon and I convinced a friend to talk to the covens about what my family was doing, what members of our community were doing. But good ol' Arthur, your ancestor, didn't care about the 'lesser covens' as they called them. He had no interest in stopping any of the buying and selling of flesh."

Astrea goes rigid. "I think I'm going to be sick." Ciaran grips her hand.

I keep going. "When Demon and I bonded, our power increased. Suddenly we were very interesting to the families. As you know, Demon was killed by the original families because we refused to join them and allow access to that power. When Lucy Carmine pulled me aside at the funeral and told me the truth of what had happened, I demanded justice. I wanted the covens to admit what they had done but no one would. That was when I went on my path of killing." I catch Demon's eyes that are shining with emotion. Even he hasn't heard the full story yet. "Agnes—"

"Fucking traitor, I knew we shouldn't have trusted her!" Demon growls, his eyes shifting to more wolf than man.

"Who was she?" Ciaran asks.

"Agnes was the only witch who I trusted at the time; she was a loner like me. Outcast by the families. Or so I thought. She was working with them the whole time. So when the spell called for a sacrifice, I slit her wrists and painted my body in the runes needed with her still-warm blood. I let her watch as the magic gathered, and in the final moments, I drove my fist through her chest and ripped her heart out." A smile spreads across my face, the delicious memory playing like a movie behind my eyes.. "It was the most blissful feeling, the way her heart still beat in my hand. Did you know the human heart can beat for a whole three to five minutes after being removed? I didn't. And it was glorious to discover that.

"The other part of the magic was sacrificing family." For a moment I'm transported back to my mother's husband screaming for mercy, my mother crying out for help. A euphoric feeling settles over me as I imagine it. Their deaths will always be my most satisfying achievements.

"Looking a little happy about murdering," Ciaran growls.

"You would be too if you knew her family," Demon replies for me.

"The Harbinger magic was fueled by all the bad that happened to me. It was forged by the anger and rage my grief was creating. Lucy either did not realize I would lose any humanity I had possessed the longer the magic was in me, or she did not care," I add, taking a sip of wine.

"Why did my ancestor even help you?" Ciaran asks before looping his arm around Astrea and pulling her tighter to him.

"Because of me," Demon rumbles. "Lucy was a close friend

of mine. She was the only one of the original family members that I spoke with."

Astrea cocks her head in curiosity. "Why? How are you connected to an original family?"

Demon and I look at each other for a moment, Demon has kept his ancestry a secret for a long time. Even when we first met, he did not share who he was and where he came from. It wasn't until after we mated for the first time that he told me. I shrug at him, letting him know it's his choice to tell them or not. It's his story, not mine.

"Lucy and I grew up together in a way. I was born into the Hoar family."

Astrea practically shoots off of Ciaran's lap. "WHAT?" she screams.

Ciaran pulls her back down onto his lap roughly as Demon gets up and pours himself more liquor. "I had a twin. When we were born, I did not appear to have magic. My family, being one of the lesser in power, decided they had no use for me. With permission from your ancestors, Astrea, they threw me to the sea. A sacrifice to the gods of old, they claimed. Thankfully Lucy's mother did not agree with it. She rescued me, and raised me in secret with Lucy."

"How did they not discover you?!" Astrea asks, the shock obvious on her face.

"I wasn't raised on coven grounds. They kept me out in a cabin, like this. It wasn't odd for Lucy's mother to wander; she often spent days or weeks away from the coven grounds. It's just who she was. So when Lucy was old enough and she began to do the same thing, no one thought anything of it. She became my best friend. She's also the reason my soul reincarnated."

I whirl my head towards him, my eyes wide. "What?"

"I was gone, for a moment. Ripped from this place and

thrown out into the universe before I was unceremoniously dumped into this wolf body."

Suddenly I wish I could thank Lucy and tell her how much it meant to me that she allowed our meeting again to happen. As if sensing my need, Demon pushes towards me and claims my mouth, his tongue sweeping in. A low moan vibrates from me.

"I truly do not want to see you fuck my sister's body," Astrea groans.

I pull back and smile sweetly at Astrea. "Guess you aren't into watching?"

"No, I just don't want to watch it happen while you are wearing my sister," she grumbles.

I laugh as Demon moves to sit back down. "Fair enough," I reply. "Anyway, the magic took on a life of its own. I didn't care. It was serving a purpose. The covens came after me, with your family at the helm of the hunt. But when they ripped my soul and magic apart, the Carmines realized they needed to create some type of failsafe should it all awaken again. Hence the magic that Kara placed in you, Ciaran. The issue is Hell magic is inherently dark – not evil per se, but dark. So the grounding they had hoped for won't work the same."

Astrea stiffens, fear passing over her face for a moment. "What do we do?"

Ciaran rubs her back gently as if her fear and anxiety are pressing down the mate bond. Her face pales, the freckles now popping out starkly. "It's okay, *Kamerate*, we'll figure it out," he murmurs lovingly.

I frown, annoyed at his disregard for her worry. "She's right to be worried, Ciaran. This magic will take over."

Demon leans forward, his leather vest pulling taught against his chest and shoulders. "What will happen if it takes over?" he asks, trying to ease my annoyance.

"The magic will allow her to act out all her desires that her humanity tells her not to. It looks different for her, I'm sure, then it did for me." A darkness moves over me for a moment, my mood souring. "I had a goal of revenge. A purpose. I'm not sure what it would do to you, Astrea."

Outside the wind kicks up, the air pushing through the small space. "Can we prevent it?" Ciaran asks over the howl.

Draining the last of my wine glass, I savor the burn coursing through me as I meander over to an old armchair. Kicking my legs and feet over the side, I stare pointedly at Astrea and Ciaran. "You need to work with me. We can't prevent the magic from doing what it was meant to do, but we can make sure you both are strong enough to bend it to your will, instead of the other way around. Otherwise," I stare directly at Astrea, "we will lose *everything*."

Demon

I wake to a warm mouth around my cock as the early light streams through the small window in the room we slept in. Looking down, Kallen's head bobs as she sucks my hard length, her ass pressed up into the air just begging to be fucked.

"Fuckkk," I groan as she swirls her tongue around my head. "You suck my cock so well." My hips jerk up, my dick hitting the back of her throat and causing her to gag. Pushing up onto her knees, she spreads her legs wide, her naked pussy gleaming in the dim morning light. Smiling wickedly, Kallen pushes her middle finger into her slick folds, pumping a few times before pulling it out and diving back into my cock. When I feel her hand start to push under my ass I lift my hips, grab a pillow, and shove it under my low back, giving her access to whatever she wants.

"So my big, bad, wolf wants my finger in his ass, huh?" she

coos as she licks me like a damn lollipop. When I feel her finger start to push in, I let out a long groan.

"Put your mouth back on my cock, Kallen, unless you want me to cum all over your face," I snarl. She laughs but listens, enveloping me again in the heat of her wet mouth. Slowly she pumps her finger in and out of me, using her own arousal as lubrication until she finds that magical spot and begins to stroke. When her tongue finally applies pressure to my piercing I let go in a shout, painting the back of her throat with my release as she fingers me through it.

When she's finally licked me clean, she pulls her finger from me and sits back up on her knees. "Good morning, *Deamhan*," she purrs.

A chuckle pulls deep from my chest. "Good morning, *Mo Chreach Bheag.*" Pushing myself up on the bed, I brush my hair out of my face before pulling it up into a bun. "Come here," I growl, beckoning her forward. She climbs on me quickly, her wet pussy lining up with my cock that is still rock hard despite having just cum. My fingers grip her hips hard as I slowly push into her. "Gods you're tight," I groan.

She bites down on her lip, her pupils blown wide. She offers up a whimper as my hand finds her clit and provides light pressure in small circles. Once I'm fully seated into her I don't move, only focusing on her clit.

"Gods damn it, Demon, fuck me," she demands, attempting to piston her hips.

I quickly pull my hand away from her clit, gripping her throat hard enough that her breathing falters for a moment. "You played with me. Now let me play with you." The hand not holding her neck tweaks her nipple. She bites her lip hard, blood pooling at the mark. Leaning up I lick the spot clean, my knot already demanding to be in her. "Ride me," I command in a throaty growl.

She does so with no hesitation, her hips undulating on my

cock as she loses herself to the sensations. I watch as she pulls up and drops down, my cock glistening in her arousal each time she lifts off me. When I finally release her throat she lets out a long moan that moves closer to a scream when my fingers go back to her clit.

"You feel so fucking good!" she cries out. "I want you to fill me up, I want to be leaking your cum all day. Fuck fuck fuck." She drags her nails down my naked chest so hard blood bubbles to the surface. In a fast move I pull her from my cock, flipping her to her hands and knees before driving my dick back inside her.

"Fuck yes, take my cock, Kallen. You look so good like this. I'm going to knot you, push so much cum inside you." I pound into her harder and harder, the bed frame creaking and hitting the wall hard.

Kallen's cunt squeezes my dick, her body tensing up as her release hits her suddenly. My knot begins to inflate and I push deep inside of her as I let my release go.

"Your knot feels so fucking good. Makes me feel so full," she groans out. Her hips push back into me as she tries to fuck herself on me. "Fuck me harder, I want to feel you all day. Make me fucking cry."

I growl and jerk Kallen up by the hair as my hand slaps her ass, the sound echoing through the room. "You want it to hurt?" I snap. I keep fucking her, the movement attempting to pull my knot from her. Her cunt stretches but refuses to let go and she lets out a long cry. I bite down hard on her neck, blood pooling from the wound as my teeth shift to allow my canines to dig into her.

She reaches back and grips my hair hard.. Her other hand grips her breast in a punishing grip, the skin no doubt bruising. "Yessss," she hisses out. I release her neck and push her back to all fours. Her fist barely lets go of my hair as I lick both my fingers and plunge them into her ass.

"DEMON!" she screams. Another orgasm rips from her body. If my knot wasn't already locking us together that one would have squirted. My fingers fuck her ass as I let her ride out the release before I pull them free and let my seed release inside her again. She finally slumps forward, the fight leaving her. Gently I roll us down to the bed so I'm spooning her, my knot still firmly in place.

Applying gentle kisses to her shoulder, my tongue passes over the bite. Her blood is still fresh on the wound.

"Mmmm. You keep doing that and I'll want to again," she groans. Her white hair has covered her face and I move the strands away so I can watch her. Her full lips are spread in a smile, eyes closed as she sinks into the feeling. "I love you," she whispers. It's rare to see her like this, relaxed and not on edge. My heart breaks thinking of why she is the way she is; even hearing a portion of her story last night shattered me.

"I love you too," I reply, kissing her temple. "You are everything to me, Kallen, *everything*. I will kill anyone, destroy every city, and go to war with whoever threatens to take you from me again. Never forget that. I will forsake my pack and club because nothing is more important to me than you. We are endgame, we've always been endgame. Nothing else matters."

She only grips me tighter.

ELEVEN

Kallen

Demon and I take turns showering in the tiny bathroom once his knot finally deflated and slipped from me. Neither of us talks about his declaration but it hangs heavy in the room. A promise that he won't be able to keep unless we save Gothic Grove. By the time I'm out of the shower he's already left our small bedroom, but his deep voice can be heard talking on the phone in the room next to ours. Leaning into the wall I press my ear against it, casually listening in.

"What the fuck was Dahlia doing there?" I hear Demon ask.

Dios lets out a sigh, his voice echoing out from the speaker. "I have no idea. I searched for her, after she left with Johnny. But she upped and vanished without a trace. I thought she was dead."

"So were the dragons hiding her?" my mate asks.

Silence. And then from Dios, "That isn't Drago's club or Shadow's, but given their mate runs it. . . maybe?"

"Rucker is going to lose his goddamn mind. He was already on thin ice; this is going to push him over the edge. We can't fucking afford him trying to go after Drago, or his mate. We'll never win that war." I hear an intake of breath before he continues. "And maybe we shouldn't win it."

"Don't you fucking say that," Dios growls, venom in his voice. "It wasn't you who helped Julian, it was your fucking father."

Demon lets out a dark chuckle. "The dragons won't see it that way. You know it and I know it. The death of his mother drove him mad, it's what allowed Alexi to get him in the first place."

Fuck, the Knights helped kill Shadows' mother? I really don't want to have to try and kill the dragons if they find out. There is no way they wouldn't seek revenge against Demon.

"I'm glad you are there at least. I mean, I would rather you be here, but with Dahlia out and about and our little visiting royal, I need someone I can trust back home," Demon says. I hear him continue to say goodbye to Dios but my mind races for a way to manage it all, to do damage control before anything can happen.

Snapping my fingers, darkness bleeds into the room. My smallest Hellbeast, a wily female I named Lark, moves out. Her twin sister, Cora, steps in just behind her. Between the two beasts, Lark is distinctive only by the white patch just above her nose. The two are so close in size that the naked eye would miss how Cora is just a tad bigger than her sister. Of all my wolves, these two are the best at finding information for me. They aren't quick to anger and prefer to stick to the shadows and observe. It's why they've also stayed with Ari the most.

Walking over, I scratch each behind the ear because despite being small, they still sit close to my chest when standing on all fours. "I need you to track Rucker. Don't kill him but keep tabs on him. I also need information on a girl, Dahlia. She's at The Playground," I croon as I step away.

Each beast backs away and fades back into the darkness, their instructions clear. Dragging a t-shirt on, I leave the bedroom in search of coffee, whistling as I go. Rounding the corner I find myself face to face with a shirtless Ciaran latched onto Astrea's neck.

"Don't mind me, just grabbing coffee," I say merrily and push past the two.

"Didn't peg you as a morning person." Ciaran's voice is still rough with sleep as he pulls away from her neck.

Spinning towards the two, coffee in hand, I offer up a smile. "Hard not to be when you wake up with a hard cock in your mouth followed by a good fucking."

"Fuck," Demon mutters as he walks in. "You have no filter, do you?"

"Nope!" I say, pushing my way out of the tiny kitchen. As I pass the Viking, I point to the side of my mouth where a small smear of blood still lays. "You missed some."

Astrea says nothing but cuts me a sharp glare as I sit down at the kitchen table.

"So what's our plan?" Demon asks. For a moment I want him to come clean; tell me what he and Dios were talking about, who Dahlia is. But he says nothing, just looks at me intently.

"Well," I start, pushing some of my hair back behind my ear. "Astrea and I have work to do. You both should probably head back to the city."

Demon growls low, the sound vibrating through our bond. "Absolutely not. And don't you even think of rolling your eyes at me over this." Ciaran snorts, earning a smack on his bare chest from Astrea.

Pushing up I walk to Demon, slipping my arms around his

massive body. "You need to go back and take care of the club. Nothing is going to happen to me here."

As if we are the only ones in the room, he brings his hands to my face. "The last time I left you I didn't see you again for decades. I can't lose you again," he pleads. His sapphire eyes swim with emotion as they lock onto mine.

"You won't," I declare. "You have two powerful witches here. Nothing is getting through to us." For a moment, Demon's gaze stays locked onto mine before he blinks away the grief and fear that were shining in them a moment ago.

"I'll be fine, my love; go hang out with Ciaran." Spinning back towards Astrea and Ciaran I smile brightly. "Alright Harbinger, let's go play!"

Astrea looks skeptical before pulling her phone from her pocket. "I'll be right back."

<hr>

Kallen

Standing in the clearing outside the cabin Astrea's hair blows in the breeze, the white and red strands floating around her face. She hastily pushes it up into a bun to keep it out of her eyes before crossing her arms over her chest and glaring at me. She's wearing an oversized sweatshirt, no doubt Ciaran's, over a pair of black leggings with combat boots. Her emerald eyes glare at me. It had taken a little bit for her to return from her phone call, but when she had, I thought her attitude had changed. Given the look I'm getting, maybe I was wrong.

"Glare all you want; it still doesn't change that you need me," I remind her.

Her nostrils flare and a hint of magic seeps from her before she shudders and pulls it back in. "I could do this on my own," she argues.

"We don't have time for that. Ava doesn't have time for that.

So if you want to help your friend, you'll suck it, buttercup." Holding my hand out I allow my own magic to unfold from me, the red mist remaining in my palm. "Copy me," I command.

She rolls her eyes but holds out her own hand and attempts to summon her magic.

The clearing turns dark, and magic bursts free of her body.

"Fuck!" I hear her growl right before the magic drops and I can see her again.

"Alright, let's try that again," I remark with a shrug.

Again and again she tries until she's a sweaty mess, the sweatshirt discarded in favor of only her sports bra. She braces her hands on her knees, panting.

"Why can't I do this?" she asks, more to herself than me.

Walking over to her I plop down on the ground, tilting my head so I can see her eyes. She startles a little and quickly moves backwards until she lowers herself onto the ground across from me. Her small fox, Poppy, walks over to her and scoots her fluffy body so she's pressed against Astrea's side.

"You can do this, but you just don't know how," I respond with genuine kindness. She gives me an exasperated look as if to say 'no shit.' I hold up my hand before she speaks. "What I mean to say is that this magic, more so than other magic, is deeply ingrained in your emotions. Unless you are calm, it's going to be more difficult to control."

"Well, I won't ever be calm around you," she counters.

"Exactly. Just like you'll never be calm in battle or if someone touches your mate. You have to operate under the assumption you'll always be triggered by something." I watch as she nibbles her lip, eyes unfocused as she thinks about what I'm saying. Now that she's holding still, I can see the faint scars on her. They've faded over time but she will always hold the mark from her time with Alexi.

"How was it I could control it when I went after Alexi?" she asks, pulling my attention back to her face.

"We can do extraordinary things in certain circumstances," I respond. "You took down Alexi's prison. I killed a lot of people who deemed themselves more powerful than I was. They learned how wrong they were, obviously." Standing, I offer my hand to her. "You don't have to like me or forgive me, but I imagine you can understand why I've done what I've done. So, if nothing else, you can trust that I want to make sure you don't go mad with this magic. Because I wouldn't wish the loss of a mate on anyone. If you go mad, that's where this ends." My words are firm but sincere. She looks at my outstretched hand for so long I almost drop it before she finally takes it and allows me to pull her to her feet. She gives me a slight nod, which is good enough for me.

Dios

Stepping back into the house, the scent of Jax immediately invades my nose, thick cedar woods and smoke dancing through the air in a tantalizing blend. I follow it through the front entry, into the kitchen and out onto the porch where I find the King staring out into the grass from his chair. A beer is held loosely in his grip, the label picked apart and illegible now.

"You're back," he says, his voice hard.

Crossing my arms I invade his space, leaning against the deck rail directly across from him. "Mmm," I say, continuing to watch his body.

"What?" He glares at me, anger shimmering beneath the surface. I only shrug as I raise an eyebrow at him. "Fine," he says after letting out a long breath. "I went and saw Ava while you were all busy."

Well there goes the plan to ask him to avoid her.

"Did it not go well?" I hedge.

Setting the beer down, he drops his head into his hands before pushing to a stand and starting to pace. "Fuck, my intent had been to bring her back home but she refused. I fucked it all up. I shouldn't have demanded she return. But seeing how low her magic was, seeing the lack of a mate bond, it just made me snap. And her fucking mate, Shadow, is a gods damn mess." His body tenses as he tries to pull back his magic. "She spent years being tortured while she was here. Years. I believed the fucking narrative my father and mother spun, that she was off partying and was just a brat."

His silver eyes catch mine. The look of sadness and desperation has me pulling his dense body into mine. For a moment he remains tense, but with one breath his muscles relax and his arms loop around my waist. "The kingdom is going to fall. I can't hold it. The Order has someone here, and they are gaining more and more followers every day. Add in the fucking creatures that are waking, and I don't even have the opportunity to unite people with me." He shudders for a moment. "It's too much. I don't want this."

Dragging his face from my chest, I hold it between both hands, "No, *mi cielo*. You can do this. You were born to lead. Your kingdom will not fall because we will not let it." I plant a hard kiss to his mouth, pulling his lip in with my teeth. He moans into my mouth, the sound ending in a whimper as I pull back. "We will get through this together. Now kneel."

Jax's face moves from terrified to calm in less then a second as his knees hit the hard wood deck. Unzipping my pants I pull my cock out, my hand stroking it roughly. "Suck," I demand. He eagerly pulls the tip of my dick between his lips. Tonguing the slit, Jax pulls more pre-cum from it. "That's it… you use your mouth so well. Keep doing it and I'll reward you," I praise on a growl. Jax moans, a hungry sound pulling from deep in his throat as he takes my full dick into him. His hands stay locked on his legs, but his fingers are white with tension.

My hips buck forward as he picks up speed, the momentum pulling a gag from Jax that makes my balls tighten up. "You want my cum? You want to taste it down your throat?" I growl.

He nods, eyes bright with need. I smile before throwing my head back and losing myself to the feeling. When my orgasm is the base of my spine I look back down at him, and when my release pulls through, my cum paints his mouth. I watch with deep satisfaction as Jax's eyes roll back in his head and the scent of his release hits my nose.

Pulling his head back but keeping my cock in his mouth, I narrow my eyes. "I didn't say you could cum, did I?" I snarl. His eyes widen in realization of the rule he broke. Pulling my cock free of his mouth I haul him upward, licking his mouth before guiding Jax back into the house and up to my bedroom.

"Come on, *mi cielo*, I want to warm my cock in your ass for the night. Think of it as extended edging for you making such a mess"

***

Demon

Drinking at the Sea Dog with Ciaran isn't as awkward as I thought it would be. I checked on the club to make sure Rucker hadn't done anything stupid, and then told Dios to keep Jax out of here. After that, I high-tailed it to the bar, needing something to calm my nerves. Despite knowing how powerful Kallen is and how capable she is, my anxiety is still high.

Ciaran drinks down the beer, his arms braced on the counter with his flannel shirt rolled up exposing his forearms and tattoos. He seems at ease despite being in a bar owned by shifters. "Why are you looking at me?" he asks, turning his cerulean gaze towards me.

"Just thinking about how relaxed you seem. Any other vampire would be on edge," I answer honestly.

He barks out a laugh. "Have you met my mate?"

I frown but nod, confused where he is going with this.

He raises a blond eyebrow. "Astrea will destroy this world if she thinks I'm in danger. So no, I'm not on edge. I've survived a lot in my time and I have a mate who might be the most powerful witch we have right now."

"It helps you also have two friends who are dragons," I retort before taking a sip of my drink.

He narrows his gaze, eyes assessing why I'm bringing up the dragons. "Aye. That's true. Want to tell me why you are bringing them up?"

Looking around the bar, there are only a handful of people here. This time of day the bar is never busy; only a small amount of the pack hanging out here. A few club whores and our old bartender are here, along with a couple playing pool at the back table. All in all, there is very little risk of talking about Dahlia. Still, something makes me hesitate to say her name out loud. As if I'll conjure up some curse of old by muttering the name of someone who should have been dead.

I can still hear Rucker screaming when he learned his baby sister was gone. The sound will haunt my dreams as long as I live. It was the moment he broke and never healed. It was the moment a lot of us broke, and had pieces of our soul scattered to the wind.

It's why I hesitate before giving a vague answer. "I need to talk to Drago about an employee at The Playground."

"No, you need to talk to Ava," Ciaran counters. "She runs The Playground. Not either of her mates. If she ever hears you say otherwise, gods help you."

Pinching the bridge of my nose, I debate on how much of our history to tell him. Why it's important that I talk to Drago and not Ava first. It's bad enough that I was at her club without declaring myself first. "My relationship with the dragons is complicated." I hope it's enough of an explanation, but Ciaran just looks at me with a bored expression painted on his face. A long groan is pulled from me. "Before I gained control of the Primal Knights, the pack used to fight in the pits. One of the people we always fought was Drago. His stepfather would bring him in, clearly drugged up, and bet money on the fights."

"Julien was a piece of shit," Ciaran growls.

I nod in agreement. "Drago came to us at one point, asking for an alliance against Julius and to save Shadow from your father. It was so early on of me taking over the pack, after my father was killed, that I wasn't thinking straight. All I knew was Julien was powerful and I was at war with another pack. I refused him. As you can imagine, relationships were strained after that." I take a deep breath. "When I was finally ready to make a deal with him, I discovered that my father had been employed by the Mori coven."

"And what exactly did they employ him for?"

I take a deep breath, praying this goes better than I think it will. "To kill Julien's wife."

For a moment Ciaran does nothing. Then he explodes, eyes red and teeth descending. His fist moves to connect with my face but I shove my body backward. "My best friend lost everything because of that!" he screams. "What the fuck!"

My wolf bristles but I will it down. "Look, I had nothing to do with it. I wasn't even President at the time. He took other members and did it behind my back. But you know what it'll look like when the dragons find out! Not only did I fight Drago in the pits, but I refused to help him. On top of that my father is the reason his mate went. . . well, how he is now."

The vampire balls his fists up, fury radiating through him before he takes a deep breath. His eyes close as he regains control of himself. When he opens they are back to blue and his fangs no longer peak out. "I'll talk to Drago for you. See if he'll meet. But aside from that, I can't force it. And I can't promise he won't try to kill you when he finds out."

I nod, thankful he'll even do that for me. Because in the end, whether Ciaran helps me or not, I have to get answers. A portal opens, my mate's magic flowing through the air as she and Astrea peer through it with wide eyes.

"We felt some toxic masculinity down the bonds. . . . anyone care to share?" Kallen asks, her eyes darting between us.

"Nah, we're good," Ciaran replies. He steps forward as Kallen meanders past him into the bar. Astrea keeps her arms crossed, her hair blowing in the soft breeze moving through the woods. The vampire plants a kiss on her forehead once he's next to her.

"Remember what we talked about, Astrea," Kallen says softly.

Astrea says nothing, only nodding before the portal closes.

TWELVE

I like Reem; she and I could be friends. But those familial bonds that are shattered broke something within her, and everyday she is slipping away. I think I'll miss her when she's finally gone.

-Personal Journal of Kallen

Kallen

The Sea Dog is quiet, the forest noises gone now that the portal is closed. Demon loops his arms around my waist. "I missed you," I say, breathing in his rich scent. My hands dip under his shirt, the thick muscles of his body greeting them. My nails lightly trace up and down, earning me a growl from him.

He tilts my chin up and grips my jaw tightly. "What do you want, my love?" His voice glides like honey over my skin.

"You," I say hungrily. "I want you, from now until always. I want to wake up stuffed full of your cum. I want to spend my days thinking about all the ways I get to worship you. I want you to fall at my feet and feast on my body like I'm your only sustenance." The longing pulls at my mate-bond, and I whine at the delicious burn.

With little thought to anyone else in the bar, Demon lets out a menacing growl before lifting me so my legs wrap around his thick center. His mouth claims my own for a moment before he walks into a back hallway, kicking open the door to an office. He lays my body down against an old wooden desk, hiking up my shirt as he does so he can draw a nipple into his mouth. He sucks it deep, teeth applying light pressure, as his other hand dives into my pants.

"So wet for me," he groans. "So needy." He presses into me with one digit before pulling out and circling my clit.

"Always," I pant. "Always needy for you. Needy for your cum and cock and hands." Pulling his hand from me he licks my arousal clean before ripping at my clothing, the offending articles falling from my body in ribbons. My own hands claw at him desperately, my core burning to get his naked body on mine. This craving has crawled beneath my skin and is eating me alive.

"I need you now," I cry. "Now, Demon, inside me. I need to feel you." He doesn't tease, sensing whatever has come over me, and sheaths himself deep within my cunt. My back arches off the wooden desk as I let out a high pitched cry.

"That's it, my good girl, fucking take my whole cock," he moans. He doesn't let me adjust, his hips unleashing as he fucks me hard and fast. His hand finds my throat and holds me down, cutting the air from me. My nails rake his arms, warm blood left behind within the scratches. A fevered energy cascading over us. His growl vibrates my whole body as he lowers his mouth to my neck, licking and sucking over my skin.

Our need for one another transcends everything; nothing else matters except for him and I. Our bodies coming together. When I feel his wolf brush up against the bond and my magic, my body tingles and my release pushes through me.

"There it is," Demon growls. I feel his knot expand, stretching the limits of what I can take as his piercing hits just the right spot. My orgasm keeps going, the waves of it pulsing through me as he cums deep within me. The desperation within our moves flashes at the edge of my mind, a reminder that this might be the last time we get to do this.

Fuck. Off.

I will away the anxious thoughts. Pushing them as far away from me as they can get, I refocus on the feel of my mate moving within me.

Demon

My knot stays firmly locked within my mate's warm pussy, each flutter of her inner walls pulling more cum from me. Her eyes are closed, sweat gleaming on her forehead, and her lips are pulled in a satisfying smile. The air around us smells like our combined release and just under it is her hint of cinnamon.

"You're beautiful," I murmur, nuzzling her with my nose.

"Mmm," she purrs while shifting her legs a bit, accidentally pulling me deeper.

I grunt in surprise. "If you keep doing that, my knot will never go down. We'll be stuck here."

She finally opens her eyes, the evergreen ringed with our silver mating bond. "You say that like it's a bad thing." Her nails lightly skim my bare chest before dragging me back down by the shoulders to plant a soft kiss on my mouth.

"You're not the one standing with their ass bare to the door," I huff out between kisses. She lets out a soft giggle, and the sound is music to my ears.

"Fine, I'll stop moving." Her hips stay still but she lets her hands memorize my body, her fingers trailing over each tattoo and scar she can reach. It's easy to forget she doesn't know this body like she knew the old one. Eventually I feel my knot deflate enough that my cock can slip free. When Kallen sits up she frowns, looking at her torn clothes. "Now what am I supposed to do?"

Rolling my eyes I grab my phone, shooting a text to Dios to come back with clothes. Pulling my jeans up, I tuck my soft cock back in before dropping the vest over my naked back. The t-shirt I had previously been wearing lay in ribbons next to Kallen's clothing. She leans back on the desk again, legs slightly spread so I can see a hint of her pussy still glistening with our combined release. When my eyes track back up, she wears a seductive grin.

"Like something you see?" She moves her milky thighs further apart, fully exposing herself to me.

A deep growl pulls from my chest, my wolf hungry and in need.

"That's right, let him out to play, baby. Let him taste me," she purrs. I watch her delicate fingers inch towards her wet cunt, my body taut with tension. She dips her fingers into the mess we left behind, head rolling against her collar bones as a pout forms on her face. "My fingers don't fill me as good as your cock. It's rather disappointing."

I snap, my knees dropping to the ground as I get ready to worship at the altar of her cunt. Her fingers drip my hair as she shoves me into her. I let her take control, fucking herself on my face. Her moans fill the air around us, louder and louder. The sounds are a joyful chorus of encouragement. In the distance I hear the door creak open.

"Dios," Kallen pants. "Care to join?"

I don't hear what he says, focusing instead on sucking her clit into my mouth while my tongue licks and circles it. Her hips pick up speed. "Oh fuck I'm close, don't stop," she cries. "Don't you dare fucking stop."

I think I hear Dios say to hurry up before the door shuts but all I care about is Kallen as she squirts into my mouth with a loud scream. I keep eating her until she rips my hair back with a growl, her pussy overstimulated now. But the satisfaction of her release dripping down my chin outweighs everything else. She pushes me backwards so she can hop off the desk, my eyes silently tracking her as she pulls on the clothing Dios brought her.

"You coming?" she asks. For a moment I want to drag her back to me and bury my cock deep within her, but a loud crash and yell have us both running towards the main bar.

Rounding the corner, I see Dios with his arms crossed over his chest and an intense look painted on his face. Following his gaze I see Jax pacing before him, the King trembling with rage.

"THAT FUCKING ASSHOLE!" he yells, flipping a table closest to him. "HE FUCKING USED ME AND HAD THE AUDACITY TO TRY FOR AVA!" His magic radiates from him, dark wings springing outward.

"*Mi cielo,*" Dios says softly. Jax whips his head toward him, his eyes no longer silver but fully black. "Breathe," Dios commands. The King narrows his eyes before taking a shuddering breath, blinking a few times as his eyes return to silver. "Talk to us."

The fight leaves Jax, his body slumping as he drops down onto a chair with his head in his hands. "Oisin, he's the one leading The Order."

"So?" Kallen hedges.

He doesn't look up, just shakes his head. "We were together for a long time. Our relationship had been off, right before Ava fled. He stuck around for a bit after but we didn't go back to how we were. Now I know why. My father had sold her to him, apparently. He was to be her fiance. FUCK." Jackson grips his hair hard before releasing again and looking up. His eyes are haunted, as if stalked by long lost memories.

"So what does this change?" I ask. Dios shoots a low growl at me before moving closer to Jax.

"What Demon is trying to say is, what does this mean for us?" she says.

Jax takes another deep breath. "Honestly? Oisin has a lot of knowledge he shouldn't. He was with me for a long time. I trusted him. It would almost be better if it was some other person from The Order." He finally pushes to a stand. "I need to go back home."

Dios grips his arm suddenly, as if he is afraid to let the King out of his sight.

"Okay," Kallen starts. She meanders over to the bar, grabbing a bottle of tequila from behind the well. "Oisin is here for Ava. I doubt he'll leave here without her, so I suggest helping her mates track the man. If you don't find him here, we'll all go to Hell."

Fear trickles through me at the idea of going to Hell with her; at the idea of potentially losing her in a fight that doesn't feel like ours. I stamp the feelings down, not allowing them to go through the bond. Dios and Jax continue to have a silent argument between them as Kallen takes sips of the liquor, watching it all with interest.

"Fine," Jax finally says. Dios' body relaxes slightly, allowing Jax to pull his arm free.

"I'll help you," Dios says quietly but Jax shakes his head.

"No, not right now. I need to do this. I'll check in later." He doesn't wait for a response, opening a portal and stepping through. When it closes swiftly behind him, Kallen whistles.

"Ooof, that was tense. Wanna talk?"

Dios shakes his head, stalking away from us without a word.

THIRTEEN

I can't do this. I know Kallen wants to figure out a way to separate us, to get her old body back and give me my life again, but I can't. I know things now that have damaged everything. I know things that, once Kallen discovers, will break me if she goes through with her plan. Yet I can't fault her for any of it.
-Personal Journal of Reem Mori

Kallen

Waiting is not a strong suit of mine. Patience is a virtue that I've never bothered to learn. So sitting here just waiting to hear from Jax, knowing what's coming, makes me want to crawl out of my skin. It doesn't help that I don't even have cock to distract me. Dios and Demon have both been busy, dealing with club politics or some shit that I genuinely don't give a fuck about. Which leaves me bored. Sure, I've searched the city, but thus far nothing has come of it. The fucker Oisin vanishing without a trace.

"Ugh, this is fucking bullshit," I say into the empty kitchen of Demon's home.

"Am I interrupting?" Jax's voice comes from behind me.

Whipping around, I find him leaning against the door jam with his arms crossed. His normally bronze skin is a shade paler and dark circles shine under his eyes. "Please tell me you have something for me to do," I beg.

He smiles; a tired one but still a smile. "You have a drink?"

I hurriedly grab us both beers from the fridge before dragging him to the living room. He slumps down in the large green armchair. "How angry do you think those dragons will be if they find out my sister is helping me behind their back?"

"Lucky for you, I don't give a shit how angry they will be," I reply nonchalantly as I lean forward on the couch. "I think I need all the details." He takes a long drink, the silence dragging. I raise my eyebrow at him and sharply continue, "Look. I've been alone a lot lately. I'm fucking dying here, so talk. now."

He laughs, another tired smile pulling at his mouth. "Ava called me, briefly sharing some of her vision with me. A calculated risk, given what can happen. She asked for my help."

"Okay…" I encourage him to continue. Kara may have shown me her vision, but they can shift. And if Ava had one of her own and is asking for her brother's help, things may have changed.

"She wants to let Oisin take her. Wants me to help her distract Drago and Shadow so she can let Oisin take her to Hell, so she can grab the grimoires." He says it rapidly, the words spilling from him like an avalanche.

Pride pulses through me for a moment at the thought of Ava taking things into her own hands. "It's smart; taking the grimoires from him would cut off some of the dangerous magic. But that doesn't eliminate the whole issue. What did you tell her?"

The devastated look on his face tells me all I need to know. "Kallen, I have to let her try. Fuck, I don't want to but I have to. Even knowing the bit I do, it feels like the only option."

I tuck my legs under me, drinking the cool beer as I think aloud. "What's your plan? It's going to take a lot to get the dragons away from her. Particularly now."

"I was hoping you'd help me." he says with a wince. "Tell them everyone is coming here, ask them to bring her."

"That's dumb. How would that distract them away from her?" I barely contain the eye roll.

He shrugs. "If they are here, with people, it'll be easier to sneak her away."

I let out a loud laugh, the sound moving through my whole body. "You don't know the dragons well. Drago will be damn near impossible to pull from Avar and if he is away, Shadow will be looming nearby. Particularly if they are mated now, which if she's making this move, I would imagine they are."

He looks at me helplessly, his silver eyes pleading for some unknown answer that he hasn't thought of.

Now I *do* roll my eyes, huffing as I set my beer down. "Look, we can't bring the dragons here. The Primal Knights won't do well with that. But I think we can send instructions to Ava. She isn't going to like this, but it's the best option." Jax raises an eyebrow, and I continue. "If she wants to pull this off, she's going to have to make the dragons believe she left them. Write a letter, leave a note, use lipstick on the mirror - I don't care. . She just has to make sure it is convincing enough for them to believe that's what is happening." I snap my fingers and Laoch moves into the room, the largest of my beasts. Grabbing a pen and paper, I scribble out a note quickly before passing it to my beast, who takes it gingerly in his mouth. Opening a portal to Ava, his giant body disappears.

"So I guess we need to figure out a plan for next steps?" Jax groans.

Pushing to a stand, I finish the last bit of my beer before going in and grabbing a fresh one. When I reappear in the living room, he looks even more exhausted. "Go get some sleep, bro. When Laoch comes back, I'll let you know okay?"

But we don't even get that far before the portal reopens and Laoch trots out with another piece of paper. Gingerly grabbing it, I open up to Ava's handwriting:

Kallen,

I know we are anything but friends; however, I want to believe in a different world we might be. It's why I'm unfairly asking for your help in all this. I'm going to Hell, and my brother is helping me. Judging by that note you sent, you are in on all this. I need this to stop before it all gets too far gone. Having seen the future, I'm sure you understand. While I plan to come back, I don't want to be naive and think I'm immune to risk of death. Shadow and Drago have one another. But my brother has no one. So my first ask is for you and your mate to help him. Don't leave him alone in his grief; he'll blame himself.

My second ask is much harder. And I know it's big.

Astrea is my best friend. She's suffered much through her life. Not dissimilar to you. It's *the similarities between the two of you that have me worried about what will happen to her if I do not come back. You are the only one who understands that magic, truly understands it. Please don't let her lose herself to it. I know I have no right to ask this and yet here I am.*

Thank you.

I blink a few times, absorbing the words on the page before looking up at Jax. "Well?" he asks expectantly.

"She was just thanking me." I come up with the lie quickly, unsure why the need to do so burns through me, aside from the fact that a place deep down in me thinks Ava knows she's not coming back. And if her brother finds out, there is no way he'll go through with this. And maybe it makes me a bad person but Ava is a big girl, and it's not my job to stop her or protect her.

I can feel Jax's eyes on me still, burning into my body as if he'll be able to see the letters printed on my soul. "You'll need us in Hell," I say, ignoring the lingering doubt on his face. "I'm bored; it'll kill two birds with one stone. I can hunt down The Order to take something off your plate, and you help with me being stuck in this house."

"What will Demon say?" A quick glare silences him, his hands raising in front of his face in surrender. "Yup, okay, sorry, dumb question," Jax stammers.

I open a portal directly to the club house. The pack turns to look at me as I poke my head through. "Come on, boys! We have things to do!" I beckon in a sinister sing-song tone.

Demon and Dios look confused, but when Jax peaks his

head around me, they walk through without a second thought.

Hell is nothing that I expected and yet everything I could possibly want. The lights and sounds overstimulate the senses just enough that I'm craving more. My eyes track the spaces around us as my boots carry me across the street, the long train of my skirt flowing behind me. The heat bites at my body that's squeezed into the black corset, but I'm so in love with the chaos the discomfort fades into the background. The strange steampunk vibe lights up a part of me that hasn't been awake in a long time.

"You look beautiful," Demon murmurs into my ear as he comes up behind me. His strong hands pull me into his body as he nuzzles my neck before letting go and standing next to me. Dios and Jax had left us alone in the city center while they did "things," both being oddly secretive about it.

"This place is brilliant," I respond, gripping his hand as I drag him towards one of the large buildings. "Let's go play!"

Demon drags me from the casino an hour later. A pout is etched across my face as we head down the street in the direction Dios had pointed us before leaving. "We need to meet up with them – we can keep playing later," he reminds me.

I roll my eyes. "Ugh... fine," I grumble. Exiting the busy streets, we meander onto a row of townhomes, each with white picket fences and no disguisable attributes. The lawns are perfectly manicured and bushes hedged just right. It's at odds with the city that lies just beyond. Demon checks his phone again before leading me towards the third one. The white fence opens from a small gate, shutting quickly behind us. As Demon raises his hand to knock, Dios answers with another man just behind him.

"Come in," he says gruffly, stepping to the side. The death god looks tired and radiates deep tension "This is Reaver," he gestures to the man in the doorframe..

Stepping over the threshold I smile at the newcomer, my eyes tracing over his massive body and snagging on the muscles and tattoos. "Well hello," I purr. Demon lets out a low growl which makes me turn towards him. "What? I can check out Dios, but not this guy?" I can't stop the smirk that pulls at my lips.

"I know Dios," Demon growls as we all settle into the living room.

"Reaver is going to help you two hunt down Order members while I help Jax," Dios explains, pointedly ignoring Demon and I's little argument.

Reavers' skin is golden, like he's spent hours in the sunshine. His dark hair sweeps past his shoulders and frames his dark eyes. His tattoos stretch over his exposed parts of his body; one cuts down from his right temple to his cheekbone. The intricate design is foreign to me; the magic simmering off him is something I've never encountered.

"I'm intrigued by you... tell me about yourself. If we are hunting alongside one another, we should get to know one another," I say. "It's rare I encounter someone with magic I don't recognize." I kick my feet up onto the table in front of me, dust falling from my dark boots.

He looks at me for a while, his eyes burning into mine intensely. "You gonna tell your pack in the shadows to play nice in the city?" he drawls.

Demon stiffens next to me as my own body goes rigid. "No one can see 'my pack,' as you call them, when they are like this." Laoch moves out of the shadows, his presence a comfort as he growls low. The rest stay in the shadows and wait to be called forward.

Reaver offers a smile, one that doesn't fully reach his eyes. "Where I'm from, those creatures of yours were often gifted to the most powerful royals. Until one day, the last remaining pack vanished. Can you imagine what day that was?" His tone is like an arctic blast.

My mouth dries up and I swallow back the discomfort at what he is insinuating. "I can't imagine what day that could be," I reply, trying to appear disinterested.

He laughs. "You are a lot of things, Harbinger. But dumb is not one of them."

"That's no longer my title, " I growl low. "My name is Kallen. If you want The Harbinger, she's in Gothic Grove. Now if you want to sit here and talk like old women, you do that. As for me? I'm ready to go on a fucking hunt."

A long pause holds the room until he lets out another deep, full laugh. "I think we are going to have a good time together."

***

Reaver

The woman, Kallen, goes about talking to her mate and Dios as I excuse myself. The presence of the creatures that follow her is unsettling. My grandmother told stories of them, as her mother had, and her mother had. All down the lines back to before they had vanished. The last pack of them, suddenly pulled away from our home, never to be seen again. It was said our family line was cursed from then on; that the creatures found a more worthy keeper.

Looking at the female, I wonder what they saw. Why was she deemed worthy and yet we were not?

My phone pings as I step into the kitchen. Jax's name flashes across the screen as I pull the phone from my pocket.

. . .

J: You good watching Kallen and Demon?

Me: Yeah, I'm good. We'll hunt down Oisin's creatures. You good?

I watch as the bubbles appear and disappear as he types. Jax isn't someone who easily allows his emotions out. It's taken years of building that trust to get him to even admit he's anxious.

J: Not really, honestly. But I can't do shit about it right now.

Me: You need to talk?

J: No.

Me: Don't do anything stupid.

J: I won't.

I huff out a snort and shake my head. He will absolutely do something stupid. Jax is a lot of things but when he gets like this, when people he loves are at risk, he tends to stop thinking and risk it all. And with no mate and no priestesses to replenish his magic, he's in a precarious place.

Shoving the phone in my pocket, my feet carry me back into the main room. "Jax needs you," I interrupt. Three heads swivel towards me but it's Dios who stands, no question in his eyes that he's who is going to Jax.

Interesting. Maybe there is something more between those two.

I glance towards the other two. "You both are coming hunting with me."

Kallen leaps to her feet with glee. "Yes! Finally! I get to kill something!" Her eyes hold a feverish glee that makes me stumble backwards briefly.

Her mate shakes his head with a smile as he stands and plants a kiss on her cheek. "So bloodthirsty." He chuckles softly before turning his attention to the other man.

He grabs Dios, pulling him into a hard hug. "Stay safe," he says gruffly, emotion clogging his throat. Magic whirls into the room, Kallen weaving it to open a portal towards Jax.

"I'll see you on the other side, Pres." Dios responds as he walks backwards, his body disappearing through the open portal.

FOURTEEN

Demon

Kallen looks gleeful as she yanks her blade from the demon's body, wiping the blood off on her leather pants. Her braided white hair has splattered gore in it, yet she looks no less radiant. Her body is a shining light in this festering place we find ourselves in. It's been a few days of hunting down creatures and trying to find information on Oisin, and hopefully this is the end of it.

I watch as she walks towards the older man tied in the center of the room. He's currently wide eyed and smells of fear and piss. The front of his khaki robe is discolored from the loss of bladder control at my mate's savage display.

"Now," she says, taking a seat on an old metal chair directly across from him. "Are you ready to talk?"

I watch him glance around nervously; he's searching, waiting, hoping that another demon will show up to save him. The safe house, if you can call it that, was clearly set up to protect important people of The Order but not to give them comfort. The molding walls, moth-eaten furniture and stained concrete floors do little to make one feel comfortable. But the amount of magic and demons guarding the place gave it away for what it was.

"No one else is coming," I say gruffly. "I can't smell any other little friends of yours."

"Not going to lie, I'm kind of disappointed in that," Kallen sighs. She's come alive over the past few days as we've hunted. The glimmer in her eyes returned; one I didn't realize had started to dim while she sat in Gothic Grove. Kallen has spent years hunting and killing, lifetimes really. And asking her to sit on her hands while I worked on club shit was a personal form of torture for her. Guilt assaults me for not realizing how miserable she had been.

"You are crazy," the man whispers, lifting his head. I shake my head, clearing it and refocusing on the here and now.

Kallen sneers, her hand gripping his throat suddenly. "Do you want to know what happened to the last people that called me crazy?" She leans in, her power melting from her into the air around us. My wolf shifts under my skin, pacing relentlessly as he watches her. The need to claim her pulsing through me. Kallen, as she is right now, is intoxicating.

"I'll give you a hint," she says in a vicious whisper. "I didn't let them go quietly."

"You'll kill me anyway." He gasps, his words being cut off by her grip around his throat.

She lets out a dark chuckle. "True. But I've spent a very long time learning incredibly creative ways to kill people. To draw out their deaths so they are begging and pleading for their lives to end. It's an art form at this point. One that I crave. So it's your choice – either cooperate or don't. I'll be happy both ways at this point."

When she squeezes his jugular a little harder he squeals, "Okay, okay! Just let me breathe for a moment!" She releases him immediately, stepping back close enough to me that I drag her body into mine, my cock rock hard against her ass.

"Oh fuck," she groans, her head falling back onto my shoulder as my hands roam across her stomach.

Nipping playfully at her neck, despite the blood, I whisper into her ear just loud enough the old man can hear. "I'm going to fuck you while his body is still warm. So be my good girl and hurry up – I want to feel you come apart under me."

"Fuck, I bet he would like to watch. He seems like a kinky fuck," she whimpers. A low moan pulls from her throat as I feel her breast through her shirt. The under-bust black corset makes it difficult to get a full handful but I do what I can. My other hand palms her sex though the leather pants, heat already radiating from her.

"If you two are almost done here, I got a lead." Reavers' voice drags me away from the tantalizing scent and feel of my mate. Kallen lets out a low growl as she glances behind us. Her body immediately begins vibrating with annoyance. "Fucking hell, make it quick," Reaver grumbles as he turns to leave the room again.

The man has seemingly gotten used to Kallen and I over the

time we've spent together. He even seems at ease around the Hellbeasts. Such a rare occurrence indeed.

Slipping my hand into the leather pants she wears, I allow her arousal to soak my finger. "You have until I get you off to get your answers. After that, it's my turn," I whisper as I plunge into her heat. She lets out a gasp as I roughly pump my two fingers in and out of her. "Always so tight," I groan.

I hear the padding of feet and my eyes catch two of her beasts heading towards the man. "That's cheating," I say quietly.

She bucks her hips forward, desperate for more friction. "You didn't give specifics of how I got the answers, lover." She lets out a squeal as I rub her clit harshly.

"You make such delicious noises, fuckkkk." I groan out as she moans. In the background the sound of screams pulls my attention back to the man.

"Well, are you going to tell me what I want to know?" Kallen pants as I re-enter her pussy with my fingers. Laoch bites down into the man's arm, his poisonous saliva dripping into the wound as the man screams in agonizing pain.

"THEY ARE IN THE PALACE!" he pants out, Laoch biting down even harder. The sound of bone crunching reverberating through the space. "Oisin is acting without the permission of The Elders, they did not agree with the overall plan. But he's going to bring us into the future." Kallen lets out a long moan, her pussy convulsing around my fingers.

"There's one," I whisper. "Do you think you can give me another? I'm feeling generous."

She whimpers, but her hips roll slowly against my fingers, allowing me to work her back up.

"What else?" she groans. "What else can you tell me? How is he bringing you into the future?"

Laoch releases the man's arm only to bite down in another spot, another scream splitting the air. "The princess! The princess – he'll use her!" he cries.

"Good boy," Kallen purrs. "Laoch, take him." Pulling my fingers from her roughly, I unbutton my own pants before shoving hers down and sheathing my cock deep within her pussy. I fuck her to the sounds of her Hellbeast ripping apart the man, his screams a symphony as our moans compete to fill the room. By the time the man is only a gurgling mass on the floor, my cock is shooting my release deep in her cunt as she squeezes down on my dick.

***

Kallen

Demon's dick slips from me, his release following as it pools into my pants that I drag back up my hips. "Well this will get uncomfortable," I grumble.

"You complaining?" He smirks at me, knowing my answer already..

I huff out a laugh, shaking my head as I turn and look at the mess of the man on the floor. Laoch sits obediently over the corpse, bits of it stuck in his mouth and fur.

"Oisin has Ava." Reavers' panicked voice booms into the space, his feet echoing through the room.

I close my eyes for a moment, taking a deep breath and willing my heart to slow and calm. When I open them again, Demon looks me over. "You knew." His tone aligns with his expression - a blank slate devoid of emotion.For a moment I feel bad that I didn't bring him into the loop on Ava's plan.

"Yes. I knew she would let herself get taken. Jax knew as well," I admit. "But this was her plan, her choice to go in and get the grimoires. I'm not going to stand in the way of someone trying to take control of their own destiny, particularly if it can save us."

A crash startles us. Glancing over, Reaver's chest heaves as he stands over the now-upended table. "I told him not to do anything stupid!" he growls. He turns and looks me directly in the eyes, spitting out, "The Harbinger is here with her mate. Jax sent her in to get Ava."

"WHAT?! Why would he do that?! We had a plan!" I yell. The rare feeling of panic pulses through me. "Astrea shouldn't be in there. We need to go. Now."

My magic flows into the room and opens a portal to the city. Screams echo out; the smell of fire and blood penetrate my nose even from here. A great roar fills the room and the sound is deafening.

"Drago" Demon breathes out.

The massive death dragon can be seen even from here, his bone body spraying black flames throughout the city. "Fuck am I happy it was Shadow who shifted last time. Going head to head with that. . . creature is not something I would want to do," I mutter.

Reaver steps forward, two blades forming from smoke. The blades serrated and menacing looking. My hand finds Demon's, my grip punishing in its hold.

Reaver turns towards us and it's only from years of seeing shit I never thought I'd see that I hold my tongue. His eyes burn red now, the irises appearing like a flickering flame. "Let's go." His words are gruff and he doesn't bother waiting as he steps forward into the crowd.

I stand frozen for a moment, the knowledge of how all this could end overwhelming me. Demon steps in front of me and forces me to meet his gaze. "We got this, *mo chech berg*. We will walk away from this." His words are fueled with love laced with a bravado I can't quite believe.

I shutter out a breath before squeezing my eyes shut. After a moment that feels like a lifetime, the emotions that were swimming through me vanish, only to be replaced by the cocky woman everyone knows. The mask that has become who I am down to the core snaps into place, and I know as I open my eyes again that they are laced with vengeance..

"Let's go raise Hell, lover," I say with a smirk.

All six of my Hellbeasts appear from the darkness, following us as we walk into the chaos unfolding. This time, there is absolutely no going back.

Harrow

(I Know Places (Taylors Version)- Taylor Swift)

My feet carry me quickly, matching the steady uptick in my heartbeat as I race down the hallway. The linen pants move around my ankles freely and the long duster jacket flows behind, exposing the thick bandeau top that braces my breasts. The chain around my belly pulls at the small piercing at my navel as it catches on the fabric. It's the only jewelry I have on me. Lady Ornate attempted to keep me as plain as she could when bringing me to court today, as she is always jealous of the affection and attention I receive from Oisin. If she were a true high priestess, she would understand *why* he will never view her as more than a tight hole to fuck.

She thinks she is so special, but she's nothing to him.

Anxiety mounts; the need to flee building in my bones as I continue towards my room. The war in my soul is constantly pulling me to run and dragging me backward to stay. The dichotomy is exhausting at this point, and I'm not sure if I'll survive it much longer. The thought of no longer being in the palace is liberating and terrifying. My life has always been lived in a gilded cage and now that I have the potential to leave… The fear is almost paralyzing.

I'm not paying attention as I round the corner, which is how I find myself falling forward, having tripped over an obstacle my distracted mind did not detect. My hands fling out, eyes squeezing shut, as I brace for the impact on the cold marble.

Warm hands grip me, pulling me back and steadying me before releasing me. Bergamot, citrus and sandalwood blend together as I inhale deeply. Slowly I blink my eyes open, glancing around the hallway. Blood paints the walls and floors in intricate designs. The artwork of it would be beautiful if it wasn't done from the gore of the guards' bodies that are ripped to shreds and strewn around the space. A gasp is dragged from my throat, the sound muffled by the mask screwed to my face.

A throat clearing startles me, bringing awareness that someone is holding my arms. Automatically my body takes a step, back involuntarily pushing into the wall and away from the unknown intruder.

"Hola," the man's voice flows roughly over my body, his form covered by deep shadows. "I won't hurt you," he assures me, taking a cautious step in my direction.

My heart picks up in tempo, practically beating out of my chest. The magic in me is desperate to escape from the metal device keeping it at bay. I feel the burn of iron as the spikes embed into my jaw to stop any chance of a scream breaking free. My eyes well, tears forming from the pain. But I'm well-practiced at swallowing it back, hiding the misery that this device inflicts upon me.

"My name is Dios." As he steps fully into the light of the hallway I can see the red blood splatter across his toffee skin. One emerald and one cerulean eye are locked onto me. His body is covered in tattoos; even his head seems to have designs etched into it. "Jax sent me." Another step towards me and he's close enough that I can smell his intoxicating fragrance under the iron once again.

He frowns, eyes tracing every inch of the mask, no doubt noting the blood that is most likely starting to escape from the iron barbs currently quelling my banshee side.

A crash and burst of screams coming from outside, drawing his attention but not mine. My focus stays locked on the predator in front of me. "We need to leave," he urges, holding out his hand to me. "Jax needs me, and I said I would get you out. So, let's go." My body stays frozen, unable to reach forward to the life line he is extending.

Or a death sentence depending on how you look at it.

"It would be very inconvenient for me to be seen here, *mi pequeña diosa.*" His voice comes out rushed, frustrated almost, as though he cannot understand why I would be hesitating.

The mask alone should be enough to say why I hesitate; let alone the reasons I keep buried deep within my heart. His aura flashes, darkness radiating from him before it pulls back in. More sounds echo through the area, closer this time, and the smell of smoke begins to fill the room.

"We really need to go," he insists again. "He sent me for you, please don't make me leave without you."

My choices are blatantly split; I either stay here and rot, or go with this stranger for a chance at a different life. Both carry a world of consequences, some potentially greater than others.*But one path will save us, save what we could have been before all this.*

That thought pushes forward, cementing my choice in the path I'm taking. Closing my eyes I let myself reach towards his hand. The moment his skin touches mine, he drags me into his body. "That's a good girl."

FIFTEEN

Dios

Nothing could have prepared me for the electricity of her skin on mine. The priestess locked behind the metal mask has me in a chokehold already. I want to curse Jax for sending me to get her; I don't want or need another obsession. Her violet eyes blink slowly as if she is coming out of a daze. When another explosion rips through the air, she startles.

"We are out of time," I say. "Let's go."

She doesn't argue as I drag her through the halls, my magic vibrating under my skin. The souls I've ripped apart are settling on me like a film I can't shake free of. Once the bodies are found, everyone will know who came calling. And when the priestess turns up missing, it won't take long for them to figure out who took her. I glance a risk behind me, her eyes darting back and forth as we race through the halls. The contraption on her face makes the violet irises more vivid.

"We'll figure out how to get that off your face, I promise." I don't think as I say it, don't question the validity of it. She doesn't react and just keeps running with me, the small drops of blood still trickling down her neck.

When we finally break out into the city the streets are full of chaos. Drago's massive dragon causes pandemonium as it flies overhead and scorches the earth. Turning to the priestess, I release her hand, "I need to let my wolf out to find Jax and my friends." She gives me a curt nod. Her eyes are hard as steel now, as if she's settled into the choice of coming with me.

My wolf bursts free, the massive creature shaking its body as it adjusts to being let loose. Immediately I scent Demon's sea salt aroma on the wind. Yet the one I'm most desperate to find is missing. For a moment I'm frozen, worry gnawing at me. Letting out a huff I desperately work towards ignoring the fact that I can't seem to smell Jax, and I let out a long howl before herding Harrow forward towards my friends.

***

Demon

(Eat the Acid- Kesha)

Everything happens faster than I can track. As soon as we step through the portal we are thrown into a fight. Creatures roam the streets along with followers of The Order and Oisin alike. It's evident they are not all one in the same. Reaver disappears in a path of bloody carnage as he rips through the enemies.

"He looks like so much fun," Kallen pouts as her whip wraps around her a demon's head, the man screaming as his demonic form flickers. Her magic pours into the instrument and the captive explodes. The debris of his body rains down around us in a shower of gore.

"Do you think we could kill in a less messier manner?" I ask as a piece of him hits my hand.

She lets out a dramatic sigh as she wraps the whip back around her body. "Ugh, fine. Party pooper." She sticks her tongue out at me, earning a growl. She winks and takes off at a run towards the next set of creatures.

"Motherfucker," I grumble before shifting into my wolf to keep up with her. On the wind I pick up Dios's scent, seemingly moving towards us. When a long howl echoes over the chaos, I breathe a sigh of relief and let out an answering crying to him. The sound is barely out of my throat before I burst into the battle that Kallen is engaging in. My massive body takes down creature after creature as my mate cuts through them next to me. It feels never ending.

When it finally breaks I stand panting, shifting back quickly as I turn and spy Dios walking up with a female. The girl's appearance pulls a deep gasp from Kallen. A metal mask affixed to her mouth with trails of blood running from it makes for a macabre appearance.

"What is that?" Kallen hisses.

"I think you mean *who*," I snort.

"This is a priestess. Jax's priestess, to be precise. Oisin put a mask on her because she's a banshee," Dios explains.

Another yell rings out and down the road I spy the next wave of problems, a seemingly never ending hoard of creatures.

"He put a fucking mask on her?" she growls low. "This fucking piece of shit put a gods damn metal mouth piece on her?"

Kallen moves to the girl, gripping the metal attached to her mouth. Fear plagues the eyes of the young priestess, tears swimming in those violet orbs. But under that? There was rage begging to be released. Pure feminine rage.

"Make them fucking pay," Kallen growls and pushes her magic into that mask, shattering the device into pieces. The gasp that comes from the girl echoes despite the noises of battle. Her mouth opens and drags in air for the first time in gods knows how long. Her long silver hair whips around her face.

"Get down," she whispers towards Kallen, who drops without a second thought. Dios and I barely make it down before she unleashes a primal scream that rips through the space beyond us. Creatures and the soldiers explode, their bodies becoming particles in the wind. Cries of pain and fear don't make it from their throats before death claims them.

The sound of her scream finally cuts off and she stands with her chest heaving as she drags more air deep into her lungs. Her eyes are wild as she takes in the damage around her. As if she had no idea what she was capable of.

"Whew. That's some fucking power!" Kallen says as she stands up, dropping the shield that I didn't even realize she put around us. No doubt if she hadn't, our ears would be bleeding out. "Do you have a name?"

The violet-eyed girl looks at my mate for so long that I think she'll say nothing. Suddenly, she utters, "Harrow." Her voice is so soft I have to strain to hear it. But Kallen has no problem, and my mate offers a wild smile to the girl.

"I think we'll get along just fine, Harrow."

Kallen

(You can't stop me- Andy Mineo)

Chaos is a drug, and I would gladly overdose on it. It's intoxicating as it runs through my body. The banshee unleashed a level of chaos that sings to me. However, the violet-eyed girl in front of me, Harrow, looks as if she is barely hanging on after using her gifts. Her body is wavering, and we need to act fast. "Dios. Get her out of here," I command.

She looks like she wants to argue with me for a moment. But Dios grips her elbow, and she doesn't put up a fight. As they turn to leave, a great roar pulls my attention from them. My eyes widen in awe and a feverish glee pushes through me when I take in what my next opponent is.

"Kallen, fall back," Demon grunts as he takes in our new foe, "we need to get out of here. NOW."

The creature stands on two legs but is crouched forward, its long arms dragging on the ground in front of it. Even not standing straight it's at least 9 feet tall, spikes protruding from its graying form. Flesh hangs off its body in patches; it's a skeletal nightmare. It lets out another screech, exposing its rotting jaw with spikes in place of its teeth and a long reptilian tongue flicking out to lick the air.

"It's an Elker," Harrow whispers.

I step forward and Demon grips my hand to stop me. My eyes shine in a frenzied glee.

"Don't even think about it, Kallen," he commands. His eyes flash, and I can tell his wolf is attempting to push out. "We need to fall back, get to Jackson and help him. We've done enough here."

Elkers are rare, coming from the most cursed place in Hell. They are nothing but rot and pain. If an Elker pierces you with a spike, you have no hope. You will die as it slowly feasts on your soul until you are a husk of human. Only then it will devour you whole. It doesn't care who is in its way; once it locks on a target it will keep going until it gets it. And right now its eyes are locked on me, my magic a beacon for it.

"Fucking hell!" Demon growls, knowing I have no interest in running. I feel the shift in him, the fur of his wolf brushing against me. His growl vibrates my soul. Creatures flee from him as his lips pull back in a menacing howl. But this foe is *mine* and mine alone.

I press up onto my tiptoes and kiss his furry snout, before I use my magic to push him back. "Go find Jackson." He lets out a loud bark as he hits the red glittering magical barrier I erect between them and me. His brilliant eyes scream I'll be punished later for this.

I turn back towards the Elker. "Keep them safe! I'll take care of this," I yell. I don't look back. I whistle and my three beasts flank me. I unfold the whip from my body, the length of it falling to the ground before my magic flows through it. Crimson, crackling power is a tantalizing sight. "Come on boys, let's go play."

The Elker screams, the noise blasting into the crowd of demons and Knights. The shrill noise is like nails on a chalkboard and any other person would cover their ears but not me – I laugh. The sound is manic and a wide smile spreads over my gore-covered face. It launches itself at me, galloping on those gangly limbs. When it reaches me, I lash my whip out. The weapon curls around its neck and sends volts through its body as I slide myself under its legs to the other side. It scrambles to get the whip from its neck, thrashing and clawing to no avail.

"You know…you kind of look like that creature from Lord of The Rings. What was it called?" I yank the whip, wrapping it around my forearm before pulling it taught and dragging the beast to the ground. "Gollum! That's what it was! But you are bigger."

I let the whip drop off its neck and it rolls itself back up before my Beast nips at its leg. The Elker flings its long arms out, narrowly missing my dog. I narrow my eyes and snap my fingers for them to back off. Grabbing a knife from one of the sheaths on my body, I send it flying out, the blade embedding into the creature's side and bringing its attention back towards me.

Its tongue flicks out towards me and I barely avoid it wrapping around my arm. "Oooohhh, spicy! That would be fun in bed!" The creature gets angrier and angrier the longer I toy with it. But how can I stop? It's intoxicating to rotate between my magic-infused whip and my knives.

"STOP PLAYING WITH IT!" Demon's voice bellows out across the space between us. I roll my eyes, but the distraction enables the Elker to slam into me. I hear Demon shout and the magic around him falters as one of those spikes drives into my arm. I grit my teeth as it sinks in, its jaw inches from my face.

"Motherfucker." I try to maneuver myself off the spike but its full body weight presses into me and that damn piece through my arm. I can feel it starting to pull at me, at my soul. "I had my soul ripped from me once, you fucker, I'm not letting it happen again." One of its hands comes around my throat, long spiny fingers closing around it and squeezing. My vision blurs and a small amount of panic starts to push through. Just as I'm about to lose the fight, a giant black form barrels into the Elker, knocking it off me.

Ripping the now broken spike out of my arm, I roll over to see my mate standing over me, lips pulled back in a growl.

I glare at the Elker as it shakes its spindly limbs and lets out another screech. My magic lashes out in a brilliant arc of crimson mist, all my rage and fury and grief from the decades pouring into it. The Elker screams, its body slowly starting to shred apart as it falls to its knees.

I watch with a large amount of satisfaction as Demon leaps forward and rips its head off with his massive jaws.

I try to ignore the burning pain where the Elker pierced my arm as I take a step towards Demon. But the sound of a dragon's haunting cry pulls me to a dead stop. My heart breaks as I listen to the mournful cry echo across the city. It's the sound I know well – grief. It drops me to my knees as if their grief is my own for a moment. Someone did not make it. My heart hammers as I catch Demon's eyes, and I only have a fraction of a second to throw my magic around us as Astrea unleashes her deadly magic from somewhere.

Pushing back up to my feet, I finally take in the carnage around us. Nothing lives. Astrea's magic has killed every single beast that was coming at us. The air is suddenly so still I worry that she's sucked all the oxygen from the world.

"So this is The Harbinger magic?" Demon whistles. "Fucking insane."

My eyes trace a path around the devastation. This magic, the magic I unleashed upon the world, is beautiful in its destruction but it's clear Astrea is losing control. Ciaran may be grounding her, helping her manage it, but the wasteland that she created here only comes from giving into the darkness. I wonder if this means she knows how good that feels. I wonder if maybe we shouldn't have brought her into this, if maybe Kara was wrong, and it would have been better that they stayed behind. Maybe we shouldn't have allowed that magic to fully awaken.

Demon slowly leans over me, covered in gore, and looks me over.

"I'm fine," I try to reassure him.

He snarls at me. "You could have died. What the fuck were you thinking?!"

My eyes narrow at him, "I was thinking I'm not fragile and could take it. Which I was doing just fine until I got distracted."

"We need to get back to the palace," Dios says, the two walking over to us. "Jackson will be worried."

I let out a long sigh, knowing what will greet us when we get there. Judging from the look on Demon's face, he knows as well.

He grips my hand hard as I drop my magic just in time to

feel a burst of wind coming from the palace. Drago's massive dragon appears next to Shadow, who is carrying a small, limp form in his arms. A portal opens, shimmering in the distance as the two walk through it.

"No." Harrow breathes out the word that is laced with grief, and I wonder how much of a relationship she had with the princess. Her violet eyes fill with tears as she watches the trio disappear. I hadn't realized Dios and Harrow were still around, and judging by the look on his face, it hadn't been his idea to still be here.

I rest my head on Demon's shoulder, taking comfort in my mate still being alive.

"Is this what Kara saw?" he asks softly.

"No. And I don't know how to feel about that."

WHAT'S NEXT?

Sneak Peak of Ruined Kingdom
A Gothic Grove Novel
Coming early 2025

PROLOGUE

My bare feet pad over the forest floor. The moss is a springy carpet that boosts my steps. In the distance I can see my mother's white hair, the color standing out brightly against her dark skin. Her eyes glance over to me; once full of bright declarations of love and joy, they seem to be cloudy a lot more recently. The man she talks to drags her attention back, frown lines deepening on her forehead.

She's always frowning now.

Ever since my last birthday, when I turned sixteen, she's been frowning.

"Lena." The soft melodic voice paints a smile on my face as I turn towards the forest. "Lena, come see me!" The voice of my mystery friend. The one who lives in the darkened wood boarding my home.

"Why can't you come here?" I whisper, praying not to draw my mother's attention.

The voice floats out again. "You know why I cannot come to your forest. But you could come here for a bit. We could finally see each other."

I nibble my fingers, a habit that my Nanna has told me to

stop more than once. The voice came to me a few days before my thirteenth birthday. I had peered into the wild wood to find a boy peering back at me. Since that day, I've spent most of my waking time sitting near the edge of this place, talking with him and confiding in him.

"Lena, we can have so much fun together. Just come here." His voice is entrancing, and something deep within me pulls towards it. A temptation. "We wouldn't have to be alone anymore." It's a game we've played for a while , and I've resisted until now.

Picking up my long skirts, I ignore the pull in my gut that tells me to remain with my mother; ignore her voice in my head telling me to remain within our own sacred wood. *You must never travel outside our forest, my dear one. This offers protection against the wild of the world that would seek to harm you.* My mother, for all that she loves me, has kept me caged here. And the urge to flee towards something new and unexpected is too great.

With her back still to me, I allow the wild part of my soul to guide me away from the safety of our land and out into the wilderness.

The moment I step over the threshold into the thick spruce trees, my feet land on hard, rock covered ground. A slight whimper pulls from me as the bare sole of my foot slips and drags against the sharp pebbles. All around me the wind picks up, a sense of dread pooling within my chest. The further I walk inward, the more nature rages around me.

I have made a mistake.

As I go to turn around, to seek refuge in the warm forest of my home, I realize just how far I've come. My mother's body is no longer in view. Instead, only miles and miles of darkened wood that seems to hold an ominous presence lie before me. The heaviness of it presses in around me. My heart beats faster, sweat prickling at my temple, and my skin feels electrified.

Every part of me is screaming to run, to get away, to escape this place. Yet my limbs are frozen, locked up and unable to move.

"Lena, you came." The voice that always tempts me sounds so close now. "I want to see you." Warmth gathers at my back as something presses into my space.

I squeeze my eyes shut. I know that if I open them, if I see the owner of that voice in front of me, everything in my world will change. For better or worse, it will all change.

"Please, Lena. I've waited so long to have you here." The pleading almost breaks me.

A warm hand pulls at my own, fingers twining with mine. Tension unfurls from my chest at the touch. Slowly blinking my eyes open, I allow my body to be turned. He was beautiful from afar, but up close he is devistatinglyhandsome. His full lips are set against a pale face, his dark hair shaggy over his eyes. The thick, corded muscles of his body bulge against the tightness of his shirt, hints of dark whirling marks peeking out of his sleeves. He offers me a dazzling smile.

"There is my Lena."

I close my eyes again at the sound of my name against his lips. The beauty of it settles into my core and awakens parts of me that I did not know existed.

"Who are you?" I finally manage to ask. The wind pushes against us, cold and angry, bringing his scent into my body.

"Yours," he responds. When he leans into my space I can feel his warm breath on my cheek. Butterflies attack my stomach as I realize this beautiful boy is going to give me my first kiss. "Always yours." He whispers this against me before tracing his mouth over mine. The light touch has me edging forward until my lips are firmly pressed against his. But as the kiss deepens, the world begins to spin on its access and darkness invades. In the blink of an eye, I'm pulled under.

Blinking my eyes open I'm met with my mother's stern face, the man she had been talking to stands directly behind her and smirks at me. The normally crisp blue sky of our wood is darkened and the smell of smoke filters into my nostrils.

"Wher—" I'm cut off, my mother roughly dragging me up from the ground. "Ouch! Mother, you're hurting me!" Her grip is punishing as her nails dig into my wrist.

She scoffs. "It's the least I can do to you for bringing this plague upon the forest. You have doomed us all." She pushes me towards a gathering of men and women at the edge of our forest. "Take her," she says, shoving me forward so hard I barely catch myself before hitting the ground.

"Mother?" Confusion emanates through me as I try to make sense of what's happening. Only a moment ago I was having my first kiss, and now...

Looking around, I finally *see* around me. Fires rage in the homes where the others have lived; women are crying huddled together, their priestess robes dirty with soot. Those images, however, are the least distressing. Nearest to where I walked into the dark woods lies a pile of dead bodies, throats slit and eyes open to the sky. I stifle a cry, my hand covering my mouth in horror.

"You had to follow that damn voice and start the prophecy." Mother growls, no longer sounding like the woman I knew prior to this. The warmth I had known all fifteen years of my life was gone the moment I turned sixteen. "You can live the rest of your days paying for that."

Thank you for reading this little novella and continuing to support me. I truly would not be here without y'all. This novella was oddly challenging for me. Kallen doesn't like to be written unless it's on her terms and let me tell you, she wasn't having it towards the end. But we did it.

Special shout out to Erin and Kristin, who both received so many unhinged voice notes from me about this book. Your encouragement and comments kept me going.

Kendra, thank you for going into this wild world with me and helping me keep track of everything. You are a gem and I'm so thankful for you and all you've done for me. Gothic Grove gets to keep growing because of you.

Also a shout out to Sam, my lovely cover artist. You keep one upping yourself with each cover you get me. Thank you for making my books so beautiful.

To my lovely husband who has, nonstop, kept me going – thank you. I love you with every fiber of my soul and these books would not be a reality without you.

And to all my readers and fans who have become unhinged for this world, THANK YOU. I cannot keep doing this without you. I love hearing from each and everyone of you so please don't stop.

Don't forget to leave a review!

Make sure to head to Goodreads and Amazon to share how you enjoyed this novella or any of the books. Reviews are so key to indie authors!

NEED MORE GOTHIC GROVE?

Make sure to stay up to date with all releases by following JA on social media. For exclusive content and art make sure to join her Patreon.

IG: PNWwritingWitch
TikTok: AuthorJA_George
Discord: https://discord.gg/XTUqUYASqe
Patreon: https://patreon.com/GothicGroveHOAs?utm_medium=unknown&utm_source=join_link&utm_campaign=creatorshare_creator&utm_content=copyLink

ABOUT THE AUTHOR

JA lives in the PNW with her partner and two gremlins. She has her own pack of Hellbeasts including a velvet hippo, a direwolf and a savannah cat. She lives for spooky season and hates the sunshine. In her house it's Halloween all year long.